Books by Oli

Arcana's Bestiary Volume 1

Arcana's Bestiary

Oliver Kerrigan

Published by Oliver Kerrigan, 2023.

Copyright

Table of Contents

The Tellier Cockatrice

Arcana's Bestiary Page 1

Magic flows through the world; a blessing from the goddess Arcana. Mankind has many names for this miraculous power – Sangterre, meaning blood of the earth, is the name that has survived the passage of time. Magic allows mankind to cast spells and enchantments. It also gives rise to monsters – the naturally occurring ones that dominate the planet's food chain and the artificially engineered ones that were once set loose upon an unsuspecting land.

1 – Le Symbole Héraldique Mort

A dead unicorn? Batel knelt to avoid the silver-stained blades of grass; unicorn blood saturated the morning dew. His regal purple magician's robe remained still despite the autumn breeze pushing against him. A frown furrowed his brow, although his youthful round face betrayed years of insightful experience. In one hand, a halberd rested; the shaft made from Sangterre-treated oak, the axe-head and spike made from steel enchanted whilst still molten in the mould. *This isn't good.* His fingertips brushed the creature's open wound taking great care to avoid any of his own chestnut-coloured hairs falling inside the flesh and contaminating the scene – he was forensic in his approach. *Deep tears from claws. Penetration from what looks like a beak. Whatever killed this unicorn drained the magic from its blood.*

'Odd the attacker didn't steal the horn,' a voice said.

Marie stood behind Batel; a blond religious cleric wearing saintly white robes with ribbons flowing from her arms. White gloves prevented her hands becoming dirtied as she clung onto a staff carved from a rare genus of mahogany grown in magical soil for centuries. A jewel at the top of the staff glistened as Sangterre flowed through it as a viscous slivery liquid, reminiscent of mercury.

'Correct,' Batel continued. *Odd the body is lying out here in open fields. Unicorns usually dwell in forests.* The majestic white steeds were the proud property of nobility; adored for everything from their cloven hooves to lions' tails. Some were even bearded, but most were shaved to maintain a perception of unambiguous beauty. The slender spiral horn was the envy of the world, a lightning rod for poachers. *Money wasn't the motivator behind this attack. The unicorn's magic was more valuable than its horn.* Batel looked behind them; a dense wood that stretched miles and miles towards the river valley stood proud in the distance. *This creature was chased out of the forest.*

'Any clues?'

It was the giant Johan. He kept watch ready to draw out his swords in case of a secondary attack from bandits. His muscles bulged around segmented body armour. Proud of his scars and unkempt beard, Johan exuded a warrior's confidence. On his back, two sheaths, secured tightly, housed swords blessed with various enchantments and designed to cut through magical defences. 'What kind of monster are we dealing with here?'

'I hope it's a gryphon!' Talitha announced.

She jumped up and down maddingly excited; she barely reached Johan's shoulders. Her hazelnut hair swished like a horse's tail. Her prize possession was a notebook detailing her adventures alongside a magical quill that secreted its own ink. On her belt, she had two daggers dipped in Sangterre ready to leave more than just a sting. A rough bag, falling apart at the seams, jumped in time with her leaps. 'Oh! Oh! A dragon? No! Maybe a wyvern!'

'Stop it!' Marie screamed, hitting the top of Talitha's head with her staff. 'Stop getting excited about random monster attacks.'

'Boring.' Ignoring the light knock, Talitha rolled her eyes. 'Besides, how many things can kill a unicorn so easily?' She scribbled away creating a makeshift bestiary.

'For a thief, you're oddly scholarly.' Marie lent on her preconceived notions before realising she had fallen for the bait.

'For a cleric, you're as uptight as I expected.' Talitha fired back her premeditated barb as soon as Marie finished the last syllable. *You're making this too easy for me.*

Marie growled incessantly. 'How can you be so rude?'

'I'll go pray for forgiveness to your goddess Arcana,' Talitha mocked whilst faking a tear with her finger. 'But I'm sure she'll agree with me.'

Johan placed his giant hand on Talitha's shoulder causing her to shiver and her spine to straighten to attention. 'Show some respect. There aren't many unicorns left.'

'Oh,' Talitha remembered. 'Should we eat it then?'

Marie furiously bonked Talitha on the head with her staff over and over again. 'What is wrong with you?'

'Stop it!' Talitha jumped backwards rubbing the top of her head. *Whose bright idea was it to give her a staff?* 'I guess leaving a unicorn to rot out here in the open is so much better than eating it.' Talitha looked around dreading there might be other predators lurking in the shadows and becoming impatient as they waited to feast.

'She's got a point.' Johan allowed his imagination to wonder. His mouth moistened; tongue jubilant at the idea of dining on the finest meat he would ever enjoy. *It would be a banquet worthy of kings.*

'Idiots!' Marie swung her staff bouncing it off Johan's sheet armour. The blow barely tickled. Johan laughed; bemused by the attempt. 'Unicorns are a protected species,' Marie shouted; she couldn't believe she found herself justifying centuries worth of tradition to simpletons.

Talitha applied some open box thinking. 'But are they protected if they're dead?'

'Batel?' No reply. 'BATEL!' Marie screeched, her voice cracking. He ignored her.

Instead, he focused on the dead unicorn and eliminated the possibilities. *What could do this? A wyvern? No beak. A gryphon? Maybe, but I need more information.* His eye caught something besides the corpse, a red feather floating in the trail of silver blood. He pierced the feather with the tip of his halberd's spike and held it aloft in the morning sunlight. *Is this from a rooster?* His mind completed the puzzle and did not enjoy the solution. His neck became stiff and he tried cracking it to relieve it. *What's a Cockatrice doing here? Either it got lost when shipped or more likely-*

'BATEL!' Marie screeched again knowing he was lost in thought. *Why can't you just listen to me for once?* 'Why did you bring this ... this-'

Talitha was intrigued, pen ready to write down the insult. 'Go on.'

'Thief!' Marie finished her sentence knowing anger had got the better of her. 'Why did you bring this thief with us? Is she really going to be useful? At least Johan is good with a sword.'

Talitha sniggered, hands on hips, chest thrown out confidently. 'Best thief money can buy.'

'We've not paid you anything,' Johan reminded.

Talitha deflated. 'Well not yet,' she laughed trying to save face. 'But if we kill a magical beast then I'll fold my gold into my bedsheets.'

'YOU ARE UNBELIEVABLY SELFISH!' Marie could not suppress her anger and frustration.

Talitha bowed mockingly. 'To balance your selflessness, I accept this heavy burden.' She sighed now, bored of meaningless bickering. *You can only win so many times.* She pointed at Batel, lost in his own world. 'Is he finished yet? What's he even looking at?'

Marie squinted to filter out the sunlight. 'It looks like a feather.'

Batel finished his examinations. 'Johan,' he ventured ignoring the bickering amongst his increasingly dysfunctional group. 'How reflective are your swords?'

Johan furrowed his brow. 'Quite.' He pulled one of the swords with its magical runes etched upon the perfectly tempered blade out of its sheath.

If the rumours are true, a Cockatrice, which is hard to kill, will supposedly die by looking at its own reflection. Problem is, out here, they aren't any mirrors. 'Pass me your sword.'

Johan consented and handed over the blade. Batel, not being a giant, struggled with its heavy weight and had difficulty lifting and moving it freely. *Remind me never to fight Johan alone.* He inspected the sword. *Not shiny enough. I can only see my eyes when the blade is up close.*

We need another means. He offered back the sword and Johan accepted it.

'Marie?' Batel explored a second avenue. 'Can you cast a mirror spell?'

'Err-' Marie grasped her staff tightly. *A mirror? I don't know if I can. That's a specific spell.* 'Why?

'We might be dealing with a Cockatrice,' Batel reported reluctantly.

Talitha cheered whilst writing furiously.

'How are we going to kill a Cockatrice?' Marie's concern was tangible.

Johan held his blade aloft championing his own skills. 'Thrust my sword through its heart!'

'I'll stab it, for an extra fee.' Talitha winked causing Marie to sneer.

Batel wondered if that would be enough. *A Cockatrice roaming free is bad news. It dirties the landscape.* 'Supposedly, it kills itself if it sees its own reflection in a mirror.'

Talitha's face scrunched in disbelief. 'Who came up with that?'

'We head towards Licorne,' Johan said; he had formulated a plan knowing Batel needed time to breathe. 'Tell them what we found.'

Marie sensed Batel's concern; he stood awkwardly; shoulders hunched. *This Cockatrice is stirring something inside him. I can see it in eyes. He wants, no, needs to be the one to stop this beast.*

Talitha didn't read the body language but was instead captivated by the idea of untold riches. 'And when we've told them, we accept the highest bidder.'

'It will probably be the Telliers,' Johan informed. 'They're local nobility.'

Telliers? Batel remembered the name. *Funders? Patrons?* 'Aren't they one of the richest families in the whole country?'

'Yes.' Marie's expression dropped realising this was probably their land. 'Unicorns are on their coat of arms.'

Johan and Talitha could see the hefty reward for removing the scourge of a foul beast that slayed the Telliers' precious unicorns, Cockatrice or not.

'And I bet they have spare treasures ripe for stealing,' Talitha said whilst she dreamt of the gemstones they had acquired either as gifts or by less morally permissible means.

'We must protect these lands,' Marie affirmed. 'The people here worship Arcana. They expect her protection.' She slammed her staff into the ground, their safety her reward.

Something's not right here. Batel was more concerned about the challenge ahead rather than any reward – monetary or spiritual. *If this Cockatrice is indeed magically enhanced, I must stop it. I've seen too many people's lives destroyed by such creatures and I've been unable to save them all. Well, that's not going to happen here.* Thinking laterally, he'd already compiled a case file in his mind; a figurative corkboard to map all the evidence. *A Cockatrice would be expensive to purchase. The Telliers could afford one, but that doesn't add up.* Buying a creature that would kill their own unicorns would be the last thing they would do.

Talitha got out one of her knives and looked enviously and longingly towards the unicorn's horn. *I'll have so much money. There's always an alchemist wanting a unicorn's horn for their crazy experiments.*

Marie grabbed Talitha by her arm, her grip surprisingly strong.

Talitha struggled. 'Let me go.'

'Touch that unicorn and I'll personally ignite your funeral pyre.' The wrath of a holy woman was one not to be tested.

Johan chuckled. 'She would as well.'

Talitha didn't reply; she realised she'd found the line in the sand and so calmly and slowly stepped back once Marie let go of her arm.

'Are you done?' Batel impatiently tapped his foot. 'It'll take all day to get to Licorne.'

'Wait a second.' Marie stood over the unicorn's corpse and pointed the orb of her staff at it. The Sangterre flowing inside the orb illuminated like a shining star in the midnight sky. The unicorn became encased in a bronze shell that sealed the body perfectly; no air would encounter it and no harm would befall it. *You can be remembered as a statue. I am so sorry.*

Batel nodded appreciatively. Johan and Talitha paid their respects. *A fitting tribute I feel.*

Batel began to lead the group to the south-west towards the base of the river valley where Licorne nestled, the image of the dead unicorn driving him forward. *We need to stop these monsters. Time to ruffle some Tellier feathers.*

2 – La Ville qui Craint le Coq Demon

The Galloping Unicorn – Licorne

The biggest inn in town was dedicated to the unicorn – wooden carvings adorned the bar and the walls were studded with an assortment of depictions, the star of which was a gigantic oil painting dedicated to the revered beast standing proud in the forest – and all of the artwork was commissioned under the patronage of the Telliers. Batel and the others stood in the corridor outside their rooms, looking down over the central railings into the open space below where drinkers raised their glasses and drank the bar dry. Batel sensed an overly happy atmosphere as if the villagers were pretending everything was fine. *Beneath the stench of beer, I can taste a palpable fear. Something's knocked this village off balance.*

Talitha was disturbed by the amount of unicorn imagery plastered everywhere. 'Are we sure these people worship Arcana? They seem to worship unicorns. I like unicorns as much as the next person, but these people love unicorns.' *Are we sure they can't legally marry unicorns here?*

'Unicorns are considered sacred by Arcana,' Marie informed her in the hope that would end the matter as she wanted to rest and be removed from Talitha's questions for a precious few hours; respite a golden luxury. *You would think she would run out of things to say, but no. The gift of speech from Arcana is unfortunately non-returnable.*

Johan noted the expensive artwork and thought a handsome payday was due. 'These Telliers definitely have full coffers.' *And they're going to be mad about the unicorn murder.*

Batel's outlook was more cynical. *The Telliers have long-reaching fingers. Their presence is everywhere in Licorne. The unicorn is their symbol and they've made it obvious who's in control.* He turned his back on the revelries to enter his room but he spotted someone in the corner of the inn, alone. *Matto?*

Without a moment's hesitation, he darted down the stairs.

'Batel?' Marie called out in surprise.

He relayed his instructions, volume diminishing as he raced away. 'Meeting. Ten minutes. Talitha's room. All of you!'

'Why my room?' Talitha whinged and made a note in her book to record her displeasure. *So much for an early night.*

Concern wrinkled Marie's face. *I've never seen him rush so quickly and suddenly before.*

Downstairs, Batel cut through the happily oblivious patrons, who laughed at his halberd before seeing its axe-head and spike. Then, they gave him a wide berth. He sat down opposite Matto before the man even had chance to put down his tankard of beer.

'Batel?' Matto recoiled. A magician, like Batel, he wore similar robes, although his were sky-blue. Tall, dark-haired, he wielded no enchanted weapons. 'What are you doing here?'

'I could ask the same,' Batel answered, placing his halberd against the table, axe-head and spike pointed towards wall. 'I doubt you're here as a tourist.'

Matto laughed ruefully. *He's as sharp as ever.* 'I'm on a job. Hunting a Cockatrice, would you believe?'

Batel inhaled deeply. He rubbed his hand through his growing stubble. *This bodes poorly.*

Matto read his body language. 'You knew?'

'We found a dead uni-' Batel bit his tongue as he realised where he was. *I don't want to be responsible for a drunken riot.* 'It was a ruthless and efficient killing.'

Matto opened his eyes wide. 'Ouch. That's going to hurt village pride if word spreads.' He swirled the remainder of his hard-earnt beer in the bottom of his tankard. 'My client has paid for a mirror shield.'

A mirror shield – would that work? Batel found the solution too elegant, but then Matto was a softer character, and one who always looked up to Batel, even now. *You followed me down this path. I inspired you. You've made no secret of that. I never had the heart to tell you no.*

'Stop!' Batel instructed. 'I don't want you to get hurt.'

'Too late,' Matto stood his ground. 'Besides, this is my chance to prove myself to you.'

Batel knew changing Matto's mind would be too difficult at this time. *He's irritatingly stubborn.* 'OK. You go after the Cockatrice.' He stood up and impatiently grabbed his halberd. 'Come on. Follow me.'

Matto downed the rest of his beverage and took a deep breath. *What have I just been dragged into?* He slammed the tankard on the table. *Good going, Matto.*

Talitha's Room – The Galloping Unicorn

Small and furnished with only the necessities – a bed and that was pretty much it – Talitha moaned about why her room was being used as the meeting room.

Marie did not help; it was her turn to tighten the highly strung spring. 'So the Tellier guards can find any incriminating evidence in your room,' she said. 'Not one of ours.'

Talitha's cheeks expanded to their maximum stretch as she puffed them out. This was all going into her notebook.

'Relax,' Johan said calmly as he leant against the wall. 'Your room is further away from the corridor, that's all. We can be more discreet in here.'

Talitha sighed out of relief. *They aren't planning to betray me.*

Batel opened the door and invited Matto into the already cramped space.

Immediately, everyone was on their guard.

Johan inspected the new arrival with a judgemental glance. He eyed his competition. Extra hands would dilute the pot of gold. 'Who's this?'

'Matto. He's an old friend,' Batel explained with the briefest amount of detail required as he rested his halberd against the wall next to Marie's staff.

Marie observed how Matto was constantly bowing in Batel's presence; it was clear to her who was the leader and who was the follower and guessed it must have always been so, even when they were kids. *Batel's never mentioned him before. Then again, Batel has barely mentioned anyone before.*

'He's already been hired to kill the Cockatrice,' Batel informed. 'He'll be useful to us.'

Matto tried to intervene but wasn't allowed a platform to air his objections. *What am I doing here? This will certainly break my client's trust.*

'So, Matto,' Batel said as he invited him forward, co-operation assumed, 'what do we know?'

Matto accepted he couldn't back out now. He cleared his throat as he composed his thoughts. 'Reports describe this Cockatrice as a beast with a rooster's head and the body of a two-legged dragon-serpent. It has attacked farms over the past few weeks, killing dogs, wolves, deer and, as of today, a unicorn. Oddly though, no chickens. In fact, it has destroyed chicken houses and many chickens have escaped. Farmers, on the other hand, have died from its vicious clawing. A local tried to fend it off with a weasel. It ate the weasel whole.'

All looked at each other, distinctively uncomfortable with the horrifying image of a killer chicken feasting upon human flesh. Matto laughed nervously. *Let's hope my mirror shield works otherwise I'll be killed by my last meal's distant cousin.*

Johan relished the chance of slaying such a bizarre yet fascinating creature. 'Sounds like a fine beast to fight.' *There will be grand tales told for years to come of my heroics. There will be songs dedicated to me.*

'Hopefully, it's just a demonic chicken,' Matto joked fretfully.

'Or a chicken dragon!' Talitha cried out in excitement as she madly scribbled everything that was being said in her notebook. All stared at her in bemusement.

Marie shook her head at her. *Why are you here?*

Talitha was about to object when- 'What?' Her notebook and quill suddenly passed through her hands as they disappeared. 'What? How?' She looked around to see where they'd gone.

On the other side of the room, they dropped into Batel's hands. He snapped the book shut. 'These were a gift, remember?'

Talitha's mouth dropped open; she was unable to form coherent words let alone coherent sentences. 'How did you-'

'Batel can create magical portals. It's his special skill.' Marie's triumphant smile shone through; this was the highlight of her day. *I've never seen such clever magic used to confiscate a stroppy child's notebook. I know I should condemn blatant misuses of magic, but Arcana's blessings come in unexpected ways.*

Talitha paused to evaluate her circumstances. *Oh my God! I'm in league with someone who can create portals. He's a thief's dream partner.*

But Johan did not care much for such tricks. *The day I can throw a sword through one, then it will be useful.*

As for Matto, he was weary of Batel's tricks. The lustre had been lost on him. *It's all fantastic until he hides your favourite toy. Come to think of it, he got away with a lot as a kid, didn't he? You should have been an entertainer rather than a monster hunter, Batel.*

'The Telliers,' Batel moved on. 'What do you know about them, Matto?'

'Apart from being extremely rich, they're currently mourning the death of the head of the family from a tragic hunting accident about a month ago.'

Batel logged the crucial information. *Does that fall into our timeframe?*

'The estate is now being run by Lord Henri, the eldest and only male heir. There are two sisters, Lady Jeanne and Lady Odette, who I'm sure, given their wealth and position, are doomed to loveless marriages where their husbands prefer chasing after handmaidens rather than paying attention to them.'

Marie's disgust at such vulgarity was entrenched. 'Marriage is a sacred bond.'

'They'll be lucky,' Talitha scoffed. 'Most of my friends growing up were the illegitimate children of the local nobility. Led to strange father issues.'

Matto got back on topic; he refused to let that nugget percolate further and disrupt his flow.

'Local rumour suggests Lady Jeanne is the brains of the family and Lord Henri is the frontman. He's not a details man.' Matto regarded how impressed everyone looked with his information and considered whether he was better suited to a career in espionage. *Certainly, as a profession, it would be less strange than trying to slay a Cockatrice.*

'OK, then. Here's the plan,' Batel said to mobilise the group. 'Johan, help Matto hunt the Cockatrice.'

'Gladly.' Johan patted Matto's back, although given his great height and colossal weight it was less of a congenial pat and more of a slam which sent Matto tripping forward, barely able to remain upright.

Balance and composure regained, Matto wondered yet again what he'd got himself into. *Why me?* Then again, Johan's enormous size, warrior-build and mentality would be a valuable ally. *Count your blessings, Matto.*

'Marie and I will visit the Telliers tomorrow,' Batel announced; he trusted Marie's compliance. She nodded her approval. 'Alright,' Batel concluded. 'Let's get some sleep.'

Johan and Matto left quickly to retire for the evening; one would dream of slaying the Cockatrice whilst the other would have nightmares of being ripped apart by the creature's beak.

'Wait!' Talitha screamed. 'What about me? What am I supposed to do?'

Batel urged patience. 'All will become clear in time.' As he spoke, her notebook and quill disappeared from his hands. This time, they fell out of a portal into Talitha's hands. Delighted, she clung onto them.

Batel picked up his halberd and smiled before bidding them goodnight. Marie was the last to leave, although not without a chastening grin and staff in hand.

Talitha crashed on her bed, fuming. *That's not fair.* She imagined the riches of the Telliers and her envy reached new heights. *The amount of wealth these nobles accumulate makes me nauseous. I wonder what Batel and Marie will find out. I want to know. I want to know now.*

3 – Le Dragon avec la Visage d'un Poulet

The Blacksmith's forge - Licorne

Johan stood in the crisp morning air and absorbed the heat emanating from the forge.

Inside, Matto collected his order; the one designed to kill a Cockatrice. Molten metal was being prepared in the furnaces and sparks flew as workmen tempered newly forged blades. *I can tell some fine weapons are made in here.* Amongst the swords being beaten into precision instruments, there had been a special order: a shield whose face was covered by a mirror. Kept as clean as possible during its preparation, it was covered in a hessian wrapping until Matto came to inspect it. *This is excellent.* He strapped the shield to his arm and fastened it tightly. *Weightier than a usual shield. But then again, mirrors are always surprisingly heavy.* He passed over the payment to the tired and sweaty blacksmith, who nodded in gratitude. Never in all his twenty years of experience had he received such a strange order.

The first thing Johan did was to observe his reflection in the shield. *Fantastic.* He tensed his muscles. He stroked his beard. He smiled, revealing his limited number of remaining teeth. All pleased him; Johan was comfortable with his body and proud of the hard-man image he projected. *Rugged handsomeness will never cease to be popular.*

Matto chuntered at him under his breath. *This exercise in vanity was a waste of time.* 'Done admiring yourself? The shield's not for you, you know?'

Johan leant forward to inspect the line of his beard.

'I know, but self-care is important. If you don't feel good about yourself, how are you going to face the monsters?'

Matto rubbed his forehead. *This is going to be a long hunt.* He decided to take charge. 'Come on, we have a Cockatrice to kill. And I want to be back by dinner.'

'Yes!' Johan declared. 'Tonight, we have roast Cockatrice!'

The Lands Around Licorne

Johan and Matto strode out across the Telliers' estate where the horses galloped freely whilst the cows and sheep grazed contentedly. Though their numbers were targeted by the Cockatrice, farm-life had to continue to feed Licorne. True, there would be less chicken than usual, but as the local butcher said, 'When you're hungry, you won't complain too much about what you force down your gullet'.

'Ah! The thrill of the hunt!' Johan enjoyed the simple pleasures in life. Out here, with his swords, he did his best work. 'Do you know how many animals I have killed, Matto?'

Matto bit his tongue. *You going to tell me anyway.*

'Well, I've lost count,' Johan chuckled. 'But monsters are my new speciality. This country is becoming plagued with them.' He paused to speculate on becoming the pioneer of a niche profession. 'In fact, one could earn a nice retirement sum killing monsters.'

'Yes, yes, if you say so.'

But Matto's irritation was lost on Johan. He was preoccupied with the mirror shield, although, in truth, the burden of Batel's expectation weighed more than the actual mass of the shield itself. *If this fails then*

Licorne is in serious trouble. And Batel will use this against me. He'll label me a fool and tell me to go home. I cannot mess this up.'

Johan itched his beard. This was quite a revelation.

'How do you know Batel?'

It was the question everyone wanted to ask.

Matto quickened his pace. *He keeps the past hidden. And so do I. No need for business partners to know you personally.* 'We're private people.'

Johan admired his honesty. 'I can respect that.'

At least he won't call me a fool, although Batel will if I fail to kill this beast. Not that I'm planning to give him the satisfaction. Matto stopped to read the lie of the land. The Cockatrice could be anywhere out here. They had to follow the trail of destruction. *Farms ransacked. Chicken coops flattened and all the chickens fled. It's like the Cockatrice is freeing them. It sees them as enslaved. Then again, the ethics of agriculture don't hold up to scrutiny.* His stomach rumbled, eager for lunch. *And that's why this debate won't happen around here.*

A fluffy white chicken brazenly approached making soft pepping and trilling noises. It marched around Johan's feet pecking at the ground for spare seeds. The giant was caught off guard. *You're a brave little one. Which farm did you flee from?* He picked up the plucky bird, his giant hands wide and strong enough to resist the bird's squirming and flailing as it squawked furiously. *Maybe I need a pet?*

'Johan?' Matto asked nervously.

Johan ignored him. *I'll call her Poulette. She'll save me money on eggs. I'll be sad when she dies, but the wake will be delicious.*

'Johan!'

Who knows? Maybe I can find a mate for you. Johan was lost in his own imagination.

'JOHAN!' Matto screamed.

'What?' Johan's voice boomed.

He looked up. 'What the-?' Shocked by what he saw, he dropped Poulette, who landed on the ground running and incessantly squawking in a disapproving tone. She scurried away, past the alpha-chicken – the Cockatrice of Licorne.

The Cockatrice was the unholy combination of an outsized golden rooster's head with a red-feathered top fused to the body of a scaly green draconic serpent. Large frilled wings sprouted from its back as if it were a real dragon. A long twisting tail swished freely and at the end of strong, muscular legs, chicken's talons staked the ground. Behind it, an entourage of free chickens, both roosters and broody hens clung close to their protector, their saviour. Matto counted their numbers. *Scores of them? Did the Cockatrice set them all free?*

The Cockatrice growled venomously before unleashing a loud roar. There was something soul-rattling about a rooster's crow amplified to the nerve-shattering, bellowing call of a dragon's bellow. Johan couldn't comprehend what he was witnessing. *This can't be natural. What sick madman thought to create this?*

He glanced towards Matto, who had equipped the mirror shield and was slowly inching forward.

The Cockatrice's tail became rigid as it whipped the ground. A small tremor reached Matto's feet. He stopped, heart banging against his ribcage. Blood pulsed frantically through the artery in his neck. *This thing could tear me apart.*

Johan's muscles tensed in anticipation of the fight. *This monster will be a worthy opponent.*

A faint murmuring began to ripple through the Cockatrice's flock as the beast stepped forward. Taller than Matto, its eyes looked down at the mirror shield, entranced by its own reflection. Its rooster head tilted and then it stood motionless. Nothing was going on behind its eyes. It stayed deathly silent for a second and then for longer and longer.

Matto dared to believe. *It worked? The mirror shield worked.*

Bemused, Johan laughed. *Well I'll be damned, killed by your own reflection.*

He was wrong.

A primal rage erupted.

The Cockatrice's beak slammed into the mirror.

It shattered.

Matto recoiled awkwardly; his balance shaken by the impact. Stray shards of glass flew high into the air. *No way! It did that with a single hit when it was standing still?* The creature hit out again. With a swipe of its talon, the mirror shield was torn clean off its handle and landed face down in the dirt.

A second swipe slashed Matto's chest.

Blood gushed out of the deep wound.

He fell back and the reaction force of the earth punched him hard.

His skeleton rattled.

The Cockatrice loomed over him.

Carefully and precisely, it placed its foot on Matto's arm and applied its full strength. The bone in his arm fractured. Matto's cries turned high-pitch and continuous, consciousness fading fast.

How can a mutated chicken be so vicious? Johan drew both enchanted swords out of their sheaths and faced the Cockatrice. *It's been trained to kill, to inflict pain.* Poulette cackled repetitively. The Cockatrice locked eyes with a new opponent. Johan grimaced. *Treasonous poultry.*

He swung one of his blades.

The Cockatrice countered by thrusting its claws forward and closing its fingers around it.

What? The sword was wrenched from Johan's hand and the Cockatrice discarded it. Its chicken followers clucked in celebration. *How can this beast be so strong?* The truth hit him. *This beast's magic must be augmenting its physical strength.* He laughed, unbelievably excited. 'A challenge!'

A chorus of blood-thirsty cries rose from the chickens, led by an enthusiastic Poulette. The beast beat its draconic wings as its roar ripped through the air.

Johan picked up his second sword and charged in. 'You are a chicken pretending to be a dragon!'

The Cockatrice tried to scratch him, but Johan positioned his shoulder, heavily armoured, to take the blow. Even so, he felt the metal dent against his skin. He slashed his sword and sliced open the scales on the beast's chest just beneath the join where the rooster ended and the draconic lizard began.

The Cockatrice recoiled hissing painfully as its chicken acolytes were silenced. Johan stood proud, grandstanding with hearty laughter. That soon stopped.

The wound started to close by itself. *Oh come on!* Then the gash vanished; the only sign of its previous existence was the stain of dried blood on the scales. *It can heal itself? Fine! I'll stab it in the heart!*

Johan plunged his blade into the Cockatrice's chest.

It staggered.

It fell backwards under its own weight, the blade still in its chest.

Johan cheered triumphantly. Then, he noticed the chickens were not mourning. Instead, they stared silently at Johan; their beady eyes judging his soul. *What?*

The Cockatrice wasn't dead. From inside the wound, Johan's blade was glowing white; its enchantment activated. *It's reacting to something. But what?*

The creature's magical defence had kicked in.

It identified a foreign object and it mobilised.

It pushed the sword out of the wound.

Despite the blade's enchantment resisting the push, slowly but surely it was expelled from the Cockatrice's flesh. It flew out at speed and clattered as it hit the ground, its white glow vanishing. The wound closed. Johan baulked. *No way? How can it possess such strong magic?*

The Cockatrice rose to its feet once again and, tail tensed, struck Johan solidly in the stomach, felling him. The evangelic chickens all cheered; Poulette clucked at the fallen giant. Johan coughed as his stomach wrenched, although the pain was secondary to the dent in his pride delivered by the demonic poultry. 'I will not be killed by my dinner!'

Getting up onto his feet, he noticed discolorations around the Cockatrice's legs and neck, just above where the rooster transitioned to the serpentine portion of its unholy body. The scales were a noticeably lighter shade of green and formed the same banded shape as the discoloured golden feathers on its neck. *It's been chained up tightly. And recently.*

'Johan,' Matto murmured.

The giant re-evaluated his priorities. *Matto's lost a lot of blood. I need to get him back to Marie.* The Cockatrice clomped forward; its beak ready to tear the giant's flesh. *But, I doubt I'll be allowed to leave.*

Suddenly, terrified cackles erupted from the Cockatrice's flock.

The creature turned its head and hissed.

A fox bold enough to sneak up from behind had killed one of the hens and was carrying it away, its neck clamped between its fangs. The Cockatrice roared and pursued with extreme prejudice.

Johan put his swords back into their sheaths.

Slowly and gently, he picked up the wounded Matto. Blood stained his huge hands. *Thank you for the distraction, soon to be dead fox.* He walked as quickly as he could without causing Matto more pain. He left behind the shattered mirror shield.

After precisely and swiftly disembowelling the once bold now deemed evolutionarily stupid fox, the Cockatrice licked its talons clean. The beast glared backwards to see the fleeing Johan. Across its blood-drenched beak and spattered feathers, the Cockatrice regarded Johan's face. It never forgot or forgave those who dared to hurt it.

4 – Le Mainor Tellier

Licorne Town Centre

'Why did you hire Talitha?' Marie complained to Batel as they marched through town, passing the locals who made way for a cleric of Arcana.

Although they respectfully bowed their heads in her presence, Marie was too busy venting to notice. 'She's immature and bound to end up in a situation that will compromise us. You may not care, but I have a reputation to uphold.' She used her staff to steady herself, and her anger.

Batel did not answer.

He simply watched the hustle and bustle of town life. He enjoyed the smell coming from the bakery, seeing chickens going to market along with their eggs and the empty church that stood tall and proud as a pillar of the community.

Yet, he couldn't shake the sense of unspoken fear amongst the locals. It clung to the air despite the fact they were carrying on with their lives pretending everything was normal. It was their eyes that betrayed them; the expression was easy to control, but eyes were gateways to the emotional state, the soul. *This is not a happy place. Something has disturbed the hearts of the people.*

'Batel?' Marie was growing impatient with him. *You have a strange outlook on the world, Batel.* 'I am talking to you!'

Batel stopped in the middle of the street. He allowed himself to be at the centre of everything for a precious few moments. It appeared her words were not filtering through. Instead, he took a moment to assess his surroundings. Then, without turning to face Marie, he issued an instruction. 'Just stand still and take it in. Just let the world flow around you.'

Marie did so.

Her viewpoint was different. *This place is alive, thriving. It needs to be protected, cared for and nurtured. It's carrying on, continuing to grow. It deserves Arcana's blessings.*

Batel, however, saw the world with more cynical eyes. He posed the riddle. 'You asked about Talitha, Marie? May I ask – where are you standing now? Where is she now?'

Marie let the sun's rays bathe her skin with their warmth. *We're out here in the sunlight. She's in the shadows.* She laughed to herself then pressed her tongue against the back of her teeth. *I see; when there's light, there's shadow.*

Batel moved on again. 'And don't worry. Your reputation will be fine. I made a promise, remember?'

Marie smiled; felt comforted. *You did.* 'Now, come on. We have some nobles to meet.'

Marie overtook Batel as he slowed down. 'You're my guard, remember? If we are to maintain appearances, you should always be behind me.'

'If you insist.' Batel cared little for formality but complied.

The Tellier Mansion

To call the Tellier home a mansion was a gross understatement; it was a castle without royal designation. The vast garden was well-tended with exotic trees and flowers from all over the country and from its colonies beyond, each finding their colourful home in this fertile and well-maintained soil. The imposing white-stone mansion stood as a symbol of power and might for all around the river valley, its castle-like ramparts tall and haughty. Batel and Marie arrived to a welcome committee. All the maids and servants bowed in Marie's presence and she reciprocated. Batel, with his halberd, drew a glance from security – men in blue and gold uniforms armed with spears. *Security is tight around here.*

'Welcome! Welcome!' Henri Tellier beckoned the cleric of Arcana and her magician guard to the front door. Robust, tall and healthy, Henri Tellier stood as a portrait definition of the ideal nobility; strong, handsome and perfectly dressed in doublet and breeches in his preferred colour – orange. Batel wasn't fooled by appearances. *How hard is it to maintain an image we all know is a lie?*

Beside him, stood an equally tall though lower-class bodyguard. His face bore the scars of a lifetime of punches, though his frame maximised strength over looks.

'Now Eric, ensure that nothing disturbs our visitors,' Henri said.

Eric grunted then departed to ensure security arrangements were kept as tight as required.

'Come in! Come in, cleric! We are grateful for your visit.' Henri allowed Marie and Batel to enter – protocol prohibited kissing the cleric's hands.

No expense was spared in the Telliers' home. They would, one day, be the envy of all the land. Kings and queens would come here for inspiration to renovate their palaces. Money was limitless and as they spent they earnt back double through their wide-ranging business portfolio. The floor was carved from wide black and white marble tiles forming a symmetrical pattern. Light filtered through stained-glass windows depicting scenes from the tales of Arcana with her unicorns, each bringing a splash of ruby or emerald or sapphire to these lavish surroundings. Batel found the excessive wealth intimidating. *They care so much for image. For control.* A marble staircase was the road up to the giant marble statue of the goddess Arcana that stood proudly at the top of the first flight and looked down at visitors. Batel made a mental note. *Better look at that later.*

Henri guided them to a meeting room. 'Come through.'

The Ladies Jeanne and Odette sat waiting; their seats placed either side of a much grander chair with sweeping diamond-encrusted arms and gold marquetry embedded into the mahogany wood. Jeanne's green eyes were fierce and precise; her long dark-blonde hair immaculately cared for. Wearing a fiery red hunting jacket and beige jodhpurs, she sat with her legs crossed. Odette shared the same dark-blonde hair, though her pale blue eyes and plain dress, together with her tendency to sit with her legs tucked back under her chair, made her appear meek in comparison to her sister.

Batel and Marie remained standing as Henri sat on his pretend throne, Jeanne on his left and Odette on his right.

'Thank you for having us,' Marie said as she bowed. Batel followed suit. 'I am Marie. And this is Batel.'

Jeanne's eyes were transfixed on Batel. *He's not your usual guard. Who carries a halberd, let alone a magically enhanced one?* She leant forward in her chair. 'We were wondering when a new priest would arrive – and preferably a younger one as the old men you send us keep dying of old age.'

'We're-' Odette dared to squeak before being silenced by Jeanne's stern glare.

Batel noted the sanction but said nothing and instead turned his attention to a giant oil painting on the wall above the fireplace of an old man sitting in the same chair Henri was sitting in now. Dressed in the same orange doublet and breeches, he bore a familial resemblance to Henri. Batel found art disconcerting. *Why are the eyes always so dead in these paintings?*

'A great man, my father,' Henri boasted. 'We are still mourning his passing. He was killed only few days ago on a hunting trip ... it was on his birthday, would you believe?' Henri forced a smile that was punctured by the irony. *Killed by what he enjoyed most.*

'I'm sorry for your loss,' Marie reassured him as part of her cleric's duties. 'He has returned to the Earth.'

Batel cleared his throat. *Enough with those pleasantries.* 'We found a dead unicorn,' he blurted. 'We suspect a Cockatrice did it.'

All the Telliers recoiled.

'Does this servant speak for you, cleric?' Henri found the break in etiquette disgraceful.

Marie cast Batel a disapproving glance. *You couldn't just play along for a minute longer, could you?* 'He's not my servant. He's my investigative partner.'

Jeanne started chuckling. 'I did think the halberd was too much compensation. He hardly seems muscular enough to be a bodyguard.' She clapped her hands enjoying the farce.

Henri shuffled his in seat. Batel noted his discomfort. *Seems Matto was right about Jeanne being the one in control.*

'Yes, the Cockatrice has been a scourge recently,' Henri admitted. 'Rather betrays the idyllic setting we have. I assume the bronze seal around the unicorn was yours?'

'Yes,' Marie admitted. 'After Batel conducted a thorough investigation. We thought it best to preserve its majesty.'

Jeanne took an interest in Batel. *He's the most interesting person to walk into this house for a long time. Intelligent, capable and I imagine quite skilled.* A small ball of fire ignited on her left middle finger. She bounced it between her fingers in a skilful, cocky display. Henri sunk in his chair, clearly intimidated. Batel noted his inferiority and the power-play as well as the zero burns on her fingers. *She's in charge. She's a talented magician.*

'So what are you, halberd-bearer?' she asked. 'A warlock? And tell me, who trained you?'

Her eyes dug into him like needles targeting pressure points. Batel felt distinctively uncomfortable; he twisted in place and tried to remain calm and composed. He felt under threat. Prey had unknowingly entered a predator's nest.

He looked around the room.

A ripe red apple sat carefree in a fruit bowl on the table next to Jeanne.

It began to roll forward and then dropped out of the bowl and onto the table before vanishing.

Moments later, it landed in the open palm of Batel's hand. He threw it into the air, watched it fall and caught it. Henri looked at Odette confused, astonished and slightly scared.

Marie glared at him; eyelids peeled back. *Showing off? Really?*

Odette was impressed, but not as much as Jeanne was; she was completely captivated and inspired. 'Oh, you're good.'

Tempted to take a bite of it, Batel thought it more impressive if he threw the apple back. Jeanne caught it with her left hand without barely moving her centre of gravity on the chair. She took the bite instead.

'What motivates a talented magician such as you to hunt such bizarre creatures?' she purred.

'That's enough!' Henri ordered. 'Are you done feeling each other's power? Or do you need a room alone together?'

Jeanne never missed a chance to patronise her brother, to remind him of the pecking order. 'Hush, brother! Those with actual magical talent are talking.'

Odette looked away, highly embarrassed. She hid her face.

Marie winced. She wanted to copy Odette's reaction. *They are not a happy family.*

Henri decided it was time to exercise a little authority. 'We will of course reward you handsomely for the Cockatrice's removal.'

At that moment, a maid brought in a silver plate laden with refreshments, trying her hardest to keep it straight. She was shaking nervously; afraid to enter.

'When did the Cockatrice–' Batel began.

The crashing of metal was followed by the shattering of glass.

'For Arcana's sake!' Jeanne rained scorn down on the crying maid.

Marie kept her eyes on the maid and saw her shaking.

'It's OK,' Henri said as he tried to calm the situation, a telling knowing in his voice, but the embarrassed maid ran out of the room. 'We're all stressed. Keeping morale high and stopping rumours has put a strain on us all.'

But Marie had noted the fear and dread in the maid's face. *That was a specific reaction.* She turned back to the Telliers. 'When did the Cockatrice start appearing?'

There was a stubborn refusal to answer. If they didn't say anything, they wouldn't be held responsible.

But Batel could see through their ploy. *They know something. Either they're scared or guilty.* He fixed his gaze upon Jeanne, who rather enjoyed the challenge. *He is someone worthy of respect and scrutiny.*

Uncomfortable, Batel ran his finger around the collar of his robe. *She's sizing me up.*

'One month ago–' Odette broke her silence. She was met by Jeanne's glare, stabbing her confidence yet again.

'Oh, who cares about some killer chicken?' Jeanne announced. 'This creature will either leave or be killed, hopefully–' She paused to look at Batel. 'By you. Ideally, it won't be long before we'll all be enjoying it together with a nice red wine sauce laughing about this sordid affair.' More pressing concerns mattered to her. The lack of concern in her voice was telling. Whatever the Telliers were hiding, information wasn't coming from her.

'This is a crisis,' Henri declared. 'Not two days after my dear father's funeral and this beast curses Licorne. Can I count on your support, cleric?'

'Have you not hired anyone already?' Marie asked, assuming that they were Matto's patrons.

'No,' Henri was ashamed to admit. His hesitation cost lives and his inaction weighed heavily on his soul.

Batel and Marie looked at each other dumbfounded. *Then, who did hire Matto?* They let the matter rest for now. This was the most they were going to get at this point. Only if the situation got worse would the full truth be revealed to them.

'This village is protected under Arcana's mercy,' Marie said. 'As her cleric, I will endeavour to ensure that the citizens are safe.' She bowed and once again Batel followed suit.

'Good! Good!' Henri sounded relieved. Odette smiled, reassured, but Jeanne's facial expression did not falter nor soften.

Henri stood up so he could escort their guests out. Jeanne kept her eyes locked on Batel. *We'll meet again.*

Henri left his sisters to their own devices and closed the door behind him. They had walked no more than a few paces when, in a gesture that took Marie by surprise, he turned to her clasped her hands, not out of lust, but in a desperate cry for compassion.

'Cleric,' he asked now they were out of earshot. 'We are without a priest. He died a week ago, of old age. And as such, I wish to receive Arcana's blessing before you depart?'

'Yes, but-' Her eyes flicked down to her hands.

Henri let go, apologising for his familiarity, but as he did so something else attracted his attention. At the top of the grand marble staircase, Batel stood in front of his father's pride and joy – the gigantic statue of the goddess Arcana.

Henri rushed to join him. 'Magnificent, isn't it?' The sculptor really captured the goddess' grace and beauty, no?'

Batel inspected the statue. Behind it, he noticed a door. There was enough space for a person to walk behind the statue and disappear. *How strange.*

He did not have time to investigate now. 'I'll remember it well,' he said, the ambiguity in his words deliberate.

Marie stood confused. *Batel's never appreciated fine art before, or statues of Arcana. What's he noticed?* Henri led Batel back down the stairs towards the cleric.

'We will meet for the blessing tomorrow noon at the church?' Henri asked.

'Yes,' Marie smiled and bowed.

Farewells said, they left the mansion – Marie with more questions than answers and Batel with more leads, more avenues to explore. *Follow the clues.*

5 – Le Pitié de l'Imbécile

Johan's Room – The Galloping Unicorn, Licorne

'Where is she?' Talitha cried. She dabbed the gaping wound on Matto's chest with a wet cloth as he lay unconscious on his bed. *The Cockatrice tore his flesh open.* 'We need Marie, she's a healer,' she said to Johan, who leant over her shoulder to see the extent of the damage. 'Where is she?'

Johan placed the back of his hand on Matto's forehead. *He's burning up. His body's not coping.* He lurched over to the far wall and punched the stone leaving an impact crater. Flakes of masonry fell to the floor. 'We were underprepared!' *I was too caught up in the thrill of battle to notice. If he dies, I shall forever be ashamed.*

The door swung open and Marie rushed in; mobilised into action.

'Where have you been?' Talitha screeched; she had seen enough blood today to last her a lifetime. She moved aside giving Marie free space in which to operate.

Marie inspected the wound. 'We haven't much time,' she whispered as she pointed her staff at the open wound, its orb touching his bloodied flesh.

Batel was last to arrive at the scene.

'Can you save him?' he asked, twisting his hands together. No reply. 'Marie, answer me!

Talitha and Johan exchanged glances; they had never seen Batel so desperate before.

Marie raised her finger; she needed quiet to be able to focus. Batel took the sign. *Hurry. Please.*

A magical light shone from the twisting, flowing Sangterre inside Marie's staff. Magic seeped through the orb's shell. It fell onto Matto's wound like stardust. It seeped into every pore and deep into the wound. Blood vessels were mended. Muscle fibres reconnected. The skin rejoined leaving only a pronounced scar and any blood still present in the wound was forced back inside. As the healing extended through his body, his limp arm now regained its strength; the bone mended.

Matto coughed violently. He lurched up in bed, panting heavily. His blood pressure shot through the roof. 'What happened?'

Marie urged quiet. She placed her palm flat against his chest to check his heart rate. 'Your body needs to recover.' From her pocket, she retrieved a small glass vial which contained a colourless elixir which was ready to be administered. 'This will help restore your stamina.' She dripped it onto Matto's lips and he drank it willingly. His face puckered; the foul bitterness of the medicinal herbs betrayed their healing qualities and it was all he could do not to spit it out. Once fully swallowed, Matto fell back and stared up at the ceiling with empty eyes.

'Rest,' Marie instructed.

'Rest?' Matto became drowsy, his body drained of energy. He closed his eyes and found peace.

Marie yawned. She needed to sit down. *That never stops being exhausting.*

'Thank goodness!' Talitha praised.

'No. Thank Arcana.'

Batel smiled; Marie's humility was touching.

'Thank you both.'

He stood over Matto's sleeping form. *You always were a fool trying to be a hero. It almost got you killed, you idiot.*

Marie grabbed Batel's hand and squeezed it. 'Don't blame yourself. It was his choice.'

Her stomach then roared. She blushed.

Johan laughed heartily. 'Healing must take a lot out of you. Come. We must eat!'

'Not before you explain what happened,' Talitha said as she prodded the giant's side. 'Is the Cockatrice dead? What about the mirror shield? I need to write these things in my notebook.'

Johan knew he couldn't stall any longer. 'The mirror shield didn't work. The Cockatrice destroyed it. It's strong. It matched my strength. I drove my blade into it. It took the blow and expelled the blade from its body before healing itself. It possesses strong magic.'

So it is magically enhanced. Batel shook his head in disbelief. 'Anything else?'

'It had been chained up for a while. There were obvious discolorations around its neck and legs.' Johan paused. He couldn't believe what he was about to tell them was the truth. 'It also has a following of bloodthirsty chickens.'

Batel scratched the back of his head. *So it was imprisoned and then set free, but from where?* He couldn't shake the feeling the Telliers had kept it somewhere in their grounds before it was set loose on an unsuspecting Licorne. *There are too many pieces to this puzzle. If the Telliers did buy it, then why? And then why release it?*

Johan slammed his fist against the wall and the whole room vibrated. 'Why didn't the mirror shield work? We were nearly killed by the Devil's roast dinner!'

'Legends are a treasure trove of misinformation. A fool's hope,' Batel concluded. He'd hoped the mirror shield would work, for Matto's sake, but his lingering doubts had been proven correct, much to his dismay. *Matto didn't deserve to be slashed open.* 'The Cockatrice was designed as a killing machine. Why would you implement an obvious weakness? Simple. You don't.'

Johan paused. He reflected on the day's event. 'When it looked at its own reflection, it stopped for a few moments and then became enraged.'

Batel exhaled. He had a small amount of sympathy for the creature. 'It was probably a normal rooster before being subjected to a horrifying, mind-splitting transformation. Now, it's lashing out at mankind. And who can blame it? Man created it, so man will pay.'

'So how do we kill it?' Talitha, pen in hand, asked the question everyone wanted to know.

They all looked at each other, lost for an answer. There appeared to be no simple solution or a miracle cure.

Marie was puzzled. 'But why kill the unicorn?'

Batel lamented. It was becoming clear the unicorn was an unfortunate victim, like the farmer and workers caught by the Cockatrice's wrath. 'It needs to feed on magic to fuel regenerative healing. Think of it like our bodies fighting infections and healing our wounds, but it uses magic instead to do it much quicker. And a unicorn is a nice, juicy package of magic. It didn't stand a chance.'

Slowly, Marie breathed in and out trying to keep focused. Healing took a lot out of her and she needed food. *There's only so much that a single creature can do on its own.*

'Then we need to keep hurting it until it runs out of magic to heal itself,' Johan concluded.

'Plus we don't know how much magic it consumes just by existing,' Marie suggested, throwing ideas out there, although she knew little about the precise mechanics of the synthesis behind magical creatures. 'A chicken and a serpent-like dragon can't be easy to keep fused together in a single body. Hardly compatible animals, you would think?'

Batel nodded in agreement. *There's no point chasing after the Cockatrice. It's fast moving. We need to find out the source of its power and formulate a plan to kill it.* He remembered Jeanne's trick with the flames. *She could be useful if push came to shove. However, she needs to be motivated to kill the Cockatrice and I got the distinct impression she didn't care about the beast's rampage.* His thoughts came back to his first suspicion. *The answers must lay in the Tellier mansion somewhere. I can't go back in. My face is known. And I can't ruin Marie's reputation.* He turned towards his hidden ace. 'Talitha?'

She leant forward eagerly. 'Yes?'

'Time for some breaking and entering.'

Talitha grinned, giddy with excitement.

Marie looked at Johan with deep concern. 'Please don't tell me-'

Batel ignored the cleric.

'Your target is the Tellier mansion.'

'Hold on!' Marie squawked.

'Find me a proof of purchase for the Cockatrice,' Batel said to Talitha. 'And only the proof.' He knew the importance of setting clear guidelines.

'I know, I know,' Talitha chuntered. *He'll throw me into the stocks if I steal anything.*

Marie slammed her staff against the floorboards. She demanded Batel's attention. 'Lord Henri seemed desperate to kill the Cockatrice. Why would the Telliers have anything to do with this?'

'They're the only ones who can afford to buy a manufactured Cockatrice and keep it chained up,' Batel reasoned.

Johan was chuffed. *My observation proved useful.*

Marie saw Batel's logic. *I'm not going to convince him otherwise.* 'OK, I'll go along with this, but where should she look? That mansion is huge.'

Batel could picture the scene perfectly. 'There's a grand statue of Arcana at the top of the main staircase. Behind it is a door. If I were a betting man, I would say that was a secret office of sorts.'

It wasn't the statue he found interesting; it was what it was obstructing. Marie found Batel's observant eye forever useful. 'But that could be a servant's door?'

'Do you think the Telliers would allow a servant's door anywhere near their priceless statue?' Batel argued. 'Think of how much traffic would be going by it.' *It might be a dead end, but it's a risk I'm willing to take.*

'Are you sure you don't want to go back yourself? I'm sure Lady Jeanne would welcome you back,' Marie teased.

Batel shivered. 'No, thank you.'

Talitha's imagination ran wild. 'Who knows? Maybe you'll be invited back to her bed chambers. Or, even better, marry her so you'll be super rich. I'll be errand girl for a fee.'

Batel snapped his fingers. 'Focus. You're after a document. Secure it. That document is more valuable to them than any gemstone. If you encounter any resistance, don't kill anyone. Just subdue them, got it?'

'Right.' Talitha understood that her daggers were to remain in her belt for the mission. *Never hurts to go in armed.* 'If I get caught murdering people, I'll definitely be executed. And then who is going to annoy Marie?' She laughed, though a nervous undertone was present. She made sure her belt was secured.

Batel mapped out the timeline. 'You strike when Lord Henri is out visiting Marie at the church for his confession. 'Just avoid the sisters. Now, go rest and prepare. I need time to think things through.'

Marie could tell Batel wanted time alone. All throughout that conservation, he kept glancing towards Matto with a deep, legitimate concern.

'I'll stay with him,' Batel informed her. 'He's my responsibility.'

Talitha rushed out to prepare eagerly for tomorrow's exploits, trying not to anticipate the riches she could steal.

Johan went to drink away his wounded pride but not before placing a reassuring hand on Batel's shoulder. 'Get some sleep.'

After they left, Marie stepped forward. 'Do you need to talk?'

'I'm fine,' Batel snapped but instantly regretted it. 'But, thanks.'

Marie bowed her head out of respect. She departed, gently closing the door behind her, and went in search of food.

Batel leant against the wall, stared up at the ceiling and moaned. He wiped his face with his free hand and bit his bottom lip. *I shouldn't have let you go, Matto. You clearly weren't prepared for this. Now, look at you. A fool who doesn't want my pity.* He glanced towards the window. *This world is polluted by madness. You and I are aware of that more than most. And here we are, hunting down an abomination that mocks any sense of normality.* He ran his fingers through his hair. *I should never have allowed you to follow in my footsteps, Matto. I vowed no-one else would get hurt by these beasts.* He went to punch the wall but stopped before inflicting pointless bruises. He lowered his hand and instead stretched and flexed his fingers. He took a seat besides Matto's bedside and kept an eye on him; the burning candle would last the night.

I want Marie, Johan and Talitha to be true allies. I truly do. I want to trust them when my life is on the line.

And so, he watched over Matto.

All night long. *Tomorrow, we bring an end to this madness.*

6 – L'Invitation du Voleur

The Stables – Tellier Mansion

Thievery never turned out to be as glamorous as it sounded in Talitha's head.

Sure, it was exciting when the adrenaline was pumping and her heart ticked faster. But then there were times when she had to bury herself inside a load of hay on the back of a horse-drawn cart and contemplate if she had made the right choices.

She spat out stray bits of dried grass that had crept into her mouth. *And this is why I never wanted to become a farmer!*

The cart stopped. The driver had left his vehicle to register his arrival at the Telliers' estate. Talitha emerged out the hay as if she was swimming the breaststroke. She leapt out of the cart and dashed immediately to the nearest storage barn where she hid in the shadows by the wall, obscured by the doors. Talitha took a moment to assess her surroundings. She noticed scratch marks on the walls. Chains lay on the floor. *What do they keep in here?* The chains glistened. *Are these infused with Sangterre? What did they need to keep locked away with such strong chains? Maybe be the Cockatrice was kept here?*

She searched her bag. *Where is it? Where is it? I hope it hasn't fallen through a hole. Ah! Got it!* A small vial contained a colourless potion. Removing the cork, Talitha drank it in one, pushing through the bitterness and burning in her throat. She tried to suppress her coughing with a few deep breaths; she couldn't be caught before the spell worked.

The enchantment refracted light around her so no man nor women could see her. First, her stomach disappeared and then, as the potion coursed through her veins, her arms and legs vanished; the tips of her fingertips were the last thing to turn invisible. *Right. I've got ten minutes. Let's go.*

Being invisible provided obvious advantages to a thief, but even so, she had to be careful. She still made noise, left footprints and could be sensed. Avoiding any growling canines on leashes was key; ninety-nine percent of the time the human handler would mock the beast for being too jumpy, but there was always one guard who would let go of the leash. Walking around guards was not optimal either because her footsteps made impressions on the earth. Avoiding splashing in puddles was critical. She had learnt that lesson the hard way.

As quietly as she could, she ran out of the barn and across the stretch of land to the main house. Two maids had stopped in front of the doorway to gossip. They selfishly blocked the entrance. Talitha tapped her invisible foot. *I haven't got time for this. Move it!* Impatience got the better of her. She picked up a nearby pebble and threw it at the wall. It rapped against the stonework and the maids looked around to see who threw it. When they saw no one, they ran away screaming. *Smooth, Talitha. Smooth.*

Now the entrance was clear, she made a dash for it. Once inside, she took extra care not to disturb anything – sliding sideways through open doors and skirting around the occasional tables laden with ornaments. *Look at the size of this place.* The scale of the manor made her feel small and insignificant; the priceless oil paintings of Telliers past looked disapprovingly down at her with their judgemental eyes. She turned her back on them and instead inspected the collection of china plates, each embellished with a unicorn. *What is it with everyone and unicorns?* She shook her head to dismiss the question; now wasn't the time to be side-tracked. *Keep moving! Keep moving!*

The statue of Arcana stood at the top of the marble staircase. It dominated the main entrance hall. *At least it isn't a unicorn.* She dashed up the stairs. *There's the door. Just like Batel said.*

Talitha tried to open it.

It wouldn't budge. *Of course not, it's locked.*

Out of her hair, she pulled a small metallic lock-pick disguised as a clip. Carefully and gently, she inserted it into the lock and turned it. She tried her best to minimise the sound. *Come on! Hurry up! Haven't got all day!* She felt herself begin to sweat. *I've only got a minute left. Come on! Come on!* Nervously checking her arms for signs the invisibility potion was wearing off, she saw patchy areas of skin reappearing. *No! It's too soon.*

She turned her attention back to the lock and tried twisting the pick again.

This time the mechanism clunked.

The door was open.

Talitha gently pushed down on the handle. The wooden door opened and she slid through the gap, closing it as quietly as she could behind her. She stood with her back straight against the wooden panels and panted heavily as the potion's effects wore off. Her body became fully visible, even the beads of sweat. *Well, at least I made it.*

Talitha took in the strange ambience of the red-walled room with its leather sofas and expensive Persian rugs. Mounted heads of hunted animals hung on the walls; some local like deer and boars, some strange exotic creatures from abroad such as lions and bears, but like the oil paintings they all had the same dead glassiness to their eyes. To the hunter, this trophy room validated their existence and boosted their ego. To Talitha, this room was a reason to apologise to the animals and she would say so in her notebook when she got chance to bring it up to date.

This was someone's study, complete with bookshelves and a globe depicting a world mapped by glory-seeking explorers. She rushed over to the desk and began to go through the various documents piled onto it looking for something of relevance. *Cockatrice? No. Something about important arms. Is this relevant? No. Seriously, they have enough money to run a small country. How do you get so much wealth? On second thoughts, I don't want to know the answer to that.*

Finally, after trawling through enough paperwork to make even court lawyers and accountants queasy, she found what she was looking for. She scanned it studiously. *Let's see. Purchase of one Cockatrice for undisclosed sum. Imported from abroad. Signature of purchaser is ... Lady Jeanne Tellier.* 'Got it!' she blurted out with fever-pitched excitement. She covered her mouth hoping no one heard and stood motionless, waiting to see if she was in the clear.

The door banged open and Eric charged in. 'Who are you?'

Talitha gulped. *This guy had to be security and by the look of him he would give Johan a good arm-wrestling match.*

He cracked his knuckles. 'You need to come with me!'

Talitha drew out the daggers from her belt.

'Now, I don't want to hurt you,' Eric insisted. 'I'll give you one more chance to surrender.' But before he finished his sentence, he charged forth. He attempted to grab Talitha within the clutches of his scarred hands.

Talitha leapt out of the way. She crashed into the bookcase. She grimaced. *Bad idea.*

Eric's reach was longer than Talitha thought. His arm grabbed her forearm and he squeezed it – hard. Talitha could feel the muscle being pressed against the bone. With her other hand, she drove the dagger into Eric's bulging, thick forearm. He cried out in agony; she withdrew her dagger and blood gushed out.

She sniggered and brandished both daggers. 'Don't test me!'

Eric roared like a wild animal. The smell of blood incensed him.

He charged. Shoulder first.

Talitha rolled out of the way.

Eric crashed into the wall, shattering the plasterwork.

He did not stagger nor show pain but instead turned to face Talitha; dust now mixed with the blood around his wound.

'Calm down!' Talitha screeched.

'You stabbed me in the arm!' Eric ran forward, swinging his arms; fists clenched and tightened.

Talitha jumped out of the way a second time and Eric crashed into the wall again. *Will you ever learn?* He breathed heavily like a hunted beast. *He can't keep this up. He's too angry. He'll leave himself open.*

Eric ran forward but this time stopped short of charging her.

He swung his fist.

Talitha ducked, dagger primed.

When she stood up again, she thrust her dagger into his side.

Eric looked down.

The blade had penetrated deep, although Talitha had taken care to avoid any vital organs. *Batel made me promise not to.*

Eric collapsed onto his knees. He applied pressure to the wound; seething, breathing, desperately trying not to go into shock.

Talitha did not want to stay around.

With the prized purchase order in hand, she dashed for the door. If she could slip away and hide, she would be able to deliver the purchase order to Batel once the coast was clear. *I'm not going to get caught! Just get to the door! That's all you have to do!*

'Look what I've found,' a confident voice said from the door.

Jeanne Tellier had caught her.

7 – Les Aveux des Coupables

The Church of Arcana – Licorne

Marie waited patiently in front of the heavy wooden doors of the local house of worship dedicated to the Goddess Arcana, the elegant spire rising high above her. She noticed the increased presence of Tellier guards patrolling the streets, ominously obvious in their blue and golden uniforms. They were here to keep the peace amongst the populace. Whispers about a killer monster in the nearby area had grown louder and fears were that one day it would come to attack this village. *Safety measures are slowly being ramped up.*

'Cleric!' Henri called out, waving at her from the far side of the town's central square. Marie waved back. 'I'm glad you came,' he said as he approached.

Marie bowed her head in acknowledgement.

Henri pushed open the doors of the empty church. Bands of sunlight highlighted the dust which littered the musty air and fell onto unicorn idols dedicated to the goddess that sat amongst unlit candles. Arcana was said to materialise in these bastions of worship once in a generation to find rest from her divine duties. Offerings from the harvest had been left at the altar for her, although it was the accepted fate of the food that the local priest would distribute it to the hungry, ill and desperate. Marie noticed the church was empty.

'How long have you been without a priest?'

'Weeks,' Henri lamented. 'The last one died of a heart attack after visiting our mansion. If I am honest, he had a terrible row with Jeanne.

It seems the stress of helping us move on from our father's death must have finished him off – he was elderly.'

Marie took a seat in the pew.

Henri kept looking at the door. He absolutely wanted them to be alone. Marie noticed his paranoia. *He must have secrets that weigh heavily.* She waited to see what he would do. Once he was convinced that no one had followed them, that there would be no one to interrupt them, he sat down beside her, although he seemed unable to speak.

Be brave, Henri. Be brave.

At first, the words came slowly. Then they raced forth. 'I must confess. We bought the Cockatrice as a birthday present for my father to hunt, but when he went to see it in the storage barn, the chain holding it was longer than he realised ... it pounced forward and killed my father with one swipe of its claw. I wanted to kill it, but it was a strange and unique creature acting in self-defence and killing it felt wrong. In my guilt and grief, I decided the beast needed to be freed, so I got one of the maids to free it during the dark of night, thinking it would leave these lands. However, I did not know the devastation it would unleash. I admit I was stupid and careless.' Henri put his head in his hands and hoped the cleric would understand. He wanted her to impart forgiveness to put an end to the countless sleepless nights he could no longer bear.

She rubbed his back. 'I have faith that the Cockatrice will be caught soon. Do not lose yours. Help heal the community.'

'Thank you.' Henri accepted Marie's kindness. 'We shall get through this.' He stood up. He recomposed himself and wiped away any stray tears, then departed ready to face the day. As he left, he was met by someone coming into the church; someone who didn't want to be spotted by her employer.

'Cherie,' Henri said and politely nodded. He left the maid to her own private prayers and reflections. He was not one to judge.

Marie thought she recognised the pale girl with mousy features. *Hold on, isn't that the maid from the manor, the one who dropped the tray? What's she doing here?*

Young, constantly nervous, Cherie automatically bowed in the presence of stronger, more confident individuals.

Marie clasped her staff more tightly. *She's heading towards me. Does she want to confess as well?*

'Are you free to talk?' Cherie asked timidly. She did not make eye contact. Her fingers fidgeted.

'Yes,' Marie said, her calm demeanour a soothing balm.

Cherie took a deep breath and calmed herself. 'I'm the one who released the Cockatrice. Lord Henri was so upset but determined to set it free. He didn't want it kept in captivity. It was strange. The creature seemed so calm when it left its prison. Peaceful. I had no idea it would rampage. So many have been hurt. Killed.' Tears fell down her cheeks; guilt stained her soul.

'I see-' Marie paused; processed. *So it was an accident then. A birthday present that went deadly wrong.* 'But why are you so afraid? If Lord Henri ordered you to free the Cockatrice, you have nothing to fear.' Marie placed a reassuring hand on Cherie's back.

'It's not the master I'm worried about. It's Lady Jeanne.' Cherie's voice trembled as she spoke. 'She didn't seem upset at all when her father died but she was furious when she found out the Cockatrice had been freed. She threatened to incinerate whoever did it.'

Marie flinched. *Incinerate? Is she so powerful?*

'I don't wish to spread rumours but I think Lady Jeanne planned her father's death,' Cherie cried.

'What makes you say that?' Marie inquired.

'Her smile.' Cherie shook her head wanting to shake the image from her head. 'I saw her smile when Lord Henri's and Lady Odette's backs were turned at the funeral. She was happy. I'm scared. I don't want to go back to the manor. Can you protect me?'

'Yes,' Marie said.

She stood up and led Cherie by the hand out of the church, impetus driving her steps. As she reached the doors, she almost broke into a run. *We've thrown Talitha into a trap.*

The Secret Office – Tellier Mansion, Licorne

'So, you found the purchase order?'

Jeanne leant against the doorframe, idly twisting her fingers to produce fire to demonstrate her magical prowess.

Talitha backstepped. *How can she do that? Batel never mentioned she was a powerful witch.*

Slowly, Jeanne walked towards her, making every footstep count. 'What sewage-ridden gutter were you conceived in?' She stood over the bleeding Eric, who reached out to her for salvation. 'Although looking at your handiwork, you're not a normal thief, are you?'

'Forgive me,' Eric cried weakly, reaching out to touch her with a bloodied hand.

'I don't forgive.' Jeanne let loose her fires upon him.

He burnt away; his cries of terror and agony snuffed out by the ravenous orange flames. There, in front of Talitha's eyes, his body disintegrated in the magical fires. Nothing remained of him; he had been disposed of in an instant. All that was left was a scorch mark on the carpet and a littering of ashes that scattered across the floor.

Jeanne mimicked washing her hands.

Talitha backed up so far she hit the wall. *I'm trapped! I'm going to die here!*

'Don't worry. He had no family. Who would marry a brute who looked like bruised potato?' Jeanne flicked her wrist. Out of her hands surged a blinding flash of light. Magical bindings wrapped around Talitha's hands then grew back into the wall and secured her tightly. Try as she might, she couldn't free herself. *I can't move.*

Jeanne sauntered forward and immediately picked up Talitha's daggers. *These nasty-looking objects could be helpful.*

Talitha tried again to free herself.

'So you bought the Cockatrice?' she said to distract her captor.

Jeanne tilted her head at her struggling prisoner in a bemused fashion. *Why do the stupid pursue pointless actions?*

'It was my late father's birthday present. He loved hunting strange and exotic things.' Jeanne pointed to the heads of the various wild animals hanging on the wall. 'He found the Cockatrice amusing before it slashed open his throat.'

'You planned that?' Talitha accused.

Jeanne laughed. 'My name is on the purchase order, isn't it? I had hoped to keep the Cockatrice as a weapon. I even had the idea of starting a collection of bizarre but deadly magically engineered predators for my amusement. But someone released it-'

'JEANNE!' Henri cried out as he came storming in the room.

Jeanne quickly turned around and hid Talitha's daggers behind her back. 'Brother?' she feigned surprise. 'Oh thank goodness. I found this thief.'

Henri saw Talitha bound and chained, and assumed what he was meant to assume. He let out a sigh of relief. 'Thank goodness you're alright,' he said. But then he noticed the massive scorch marks on the expensive red carpet. 'What happened? Have you seen Odette? Where's Eric?'

Jeanne didn't reply, not directly.

'Enjoy your talk with the cleric?' she asked.

Henri's eyes flicked from the sight of Talitha bound to the wall to the massive scorch mark.

'I confessed,' he blurted.

Jeanne slapped him across the face with her free hand. 'What did you tell the cleric?'

'I told her that we bought the Cockatrice. I told her I freed it.'

'You did what?' she asked, the twitch in her eyelid unmistakable. *You colossal idiot!* 'You released a designer magical beast into the wild?'

'Wait … you knew what it was capable of?'

Jeanne glared at him. 'Of course I did, I bought it!'

Henri didn't know what to say, or do. He was in too deep to be able to walk away from this and yet he knew someone was going to have to do something to cover their tracks.

'We can fix this, right?'

Jeanne readied her knife behind her back.

'I can. Yes,'

'NO!' Talitha cried out in warning.

But it was too late.

Henri let out a low groan.

Jeanne had forced one of Talitha's daggers into his chest. The blade cut through his muscles and dug into his vital organs.

He reached out towards Jeanne, who withdrew the blade and knocked his hand away.

He stared at her in disbelief then slumped to the floor as Jeanne stood quietly by and wiped the blood from the dagger.

'Thank you, thief,' she said. 'You've been more useful than I realised. I have someone who is going to be executed for murder. On top of that, I can blame you for setting the Cockatrice loose.' Jeanne pricked her own finger with the point of Talitha's dagger and laughed with the arrogance of a woman who knew she would be believed.

Even if Talitha screamed to the masses what she had seen, she would be ignored and be charged with perverting the course of justice out of spite from the local judges, who would already have received a generous donation for their judgments.

Talitha fought to break free but to no avail. 'You killed your own brother?'

'I'd just finished explaining how I planned patricide, so you think fratricide is beyond me? Is naivety contagious?'

Jeanne looked over her shoulder; she rather hoped Odette would wander in and make this the most convenient day ever. *She'll be here soon enough.* Right now, she would savour the moment. She rolled her shoulders and felt the muscles release. *I'm free. Free from forever living in my lesser sibling's shadow. This family is mine now, father!*

'Your mother would be horrified,' Talitha screeched before realising the truth. 'You killed her too, didn't you?'

'She taught me everything I knew. So proud. So wise. Though that's the tragedy of motherhood, you give birth to your own replacements.' Jeanne stared at her brother's corpse and lamented the funeral costs. *Much wiser investments could be made, but appearances must be maintained.*

Talitha knew she had one last card to play.

'I'm not alone,' she said. 'I've got allies. They'll come and find me.'

'These allies, they wouldn't happen to be Batel and that cleric, would they?'

Jeanne sounded excited, too excited.

'Um-' Talitha bit her tongue.

'Good. Let them come. I look forward to it.' Jeanne delivered a swift blow to Talitha's neck.

She lost consciousness.

She wasn't dead. No, she was still useful. *Let's see what falls for the bait.*

Batel's Room – The Galloping Unicorn, Licorne

'Talitha's in danger.'

Marie stormed in through the door, slamming it against the stone wall so that its frame shook. She did not care if she woke Matto, who was still sleeping in Batel's bed.

'What? Where?' he mumbled as he put his hand to his head; he had one almighty headache.

Batel, who had remained on watch, jumped up and grabbed his halberd.

'Don't worry, Matto, I'll deal with this.' He turned to Marie. 'What's happened?'

Marie stepped to one side to reveal a reluctant Cherie cowering in the shadows. Batel raised his eyebrows. *That's the maid who dropped the tray, isn't it? What's she doing here?*

Marie told him the story – as Henri had told it to her.

'He admitted they bought the Cockatrice as a birthday present for their late father but said they didn't know it was a killer. He ordered the release of the beast not realising what it was capable of.' She paused. 'But Cherie here suspects it wasn't a tragic accident, at all.'

'Lady Jeanne.' Batel's mind leapt to its own conclusion. 'Oh no, Talitha ... Cherie, stay here. Look after our patient.'

Matto whinged incoherently. Cherie nodded; her orders understood.

'I'll come with you,' Marie volunteered. Batel flashed her a glance. 'I know I despise her but that doesn't mean I can't save her.'

'I'll tell her that,' he joked.

He passed his fingers over the halberd's axe-head and then slashed his weapon through the air. A ripple travelled across the room and hit the wall, which became like fluid, ebbing and flowing around a central point.

Cherie covered her mouth in shock. 'Incredible!'

'You created a long-range portal – I thought that was for emergencies only?' Marie enquired.

'This counts as an emergency,' Batel affirmed.

He stumbled forwards, exhausted from the exertion.

Marie caught him.

It took a moment for him to compose himself and stand on his own two feet again. Marie understood; she knew how much magic it took to conjure up a large portal – the cost was severe and repetitive use was ill-advised. 'Have you got enough magic left to see this through?' she asked.

'Enough for one more portal if needed. Now let's go, we don't have time to lose.'

8 – Le Manifeste de la Sorcèrie

Batel's Room – The Galloping Unicorn

A knock on the door. Matto sat up in bed to see Cherie pacing around the room. Before either of them had chance to speak, the door burst open and a woman in a black hooded cloak charged in. Without a word, she took down her hood to reveal long flowing hair and the expression of someone who had had enough of other people's incompetence.

'Mistress?' Cherie backstepped, bowed.

Odette's face scrunched in confusion.

'What are you doing here?'

'I-' Cherie couldn't think on the fly.

'Don't worry. It doesn't matter. I'm not here to see you.' Odette rushed to Matto's bedside. 'Did it work?'

'Did what work?'

Odette slapped his face; she found his confusion supremely infuriating. 'The mirror shield! Did the mirror shield work? Is the Cockatrice dead?'

Matto pieced the clues together. 'You're my client?'

She slapped him again. 'Yes. Henri wouldn't do anything to put a stop to the creature because Jeanne controls everything. So, I acted discreetly. I made my own plan. Now, tell me, is the beast dead?'

'No. It broke the shield and nearly killed me.' She slapped him a third time. Matto rubbed his face, the stinging relentless. 'Why do you keep hitting me?'

She took a step back; took a deep breath.

'My father's been killed by a demonic chicken,' she squealed, her voice rising as she spoke, 'an act for which my sister is most likely responsible and from which I can only conclude that she probably wants me dead too, so all in all I have a bit of a short fuse!'

Matto glanced towards Cherie. *Come on. I need help here.*

'It's OK,' Cherie rushed to comfort her employer. 'The cleric will protect us. She and the magician are going to end this madness.'

'Good.' Odette sat down and looked at Matto 'Sorry, I lost control.' She blew her nose on an embroidered handkerchief. 'I know it's not your fault.'

Matto was too scared to speak. He nodded slowly. *I should never have come to Licorne.*

'I'm staying here,' Odette insisted. 'Where I'm safe from my sister's reach.'

Cherie curtseyed. 'Of course, madam.'

Matto nursed his face. *Oh Arcana, help me.*

'Do you think the cleric can defeat my sister?' Odette asked. 'She casts powerful fire and binding spells.'

Cherie did not know. She flinched at the thought of facing Jeanne's wrath.

Matto stared at the wall that only minutes earlier was a portal. 'Batel is one of the most talented magicians I know. He'll find a way.'

The Garden – The Tellier Mansion

The bronze unicorn had been placed on a stone pedestal in the centre of the garden as a memorial to the recently deceased animal. Henri had thought it appropriate. It turned out to be the last noteworthy deed he ever commissioned. There hadn't been time to engrave a plaque, so instead, in its honour, Jeanne decided to chain an unconscious Talitha to the base of the monument with her magical bindings.

It was at this moment that Batel and Marie came running down the garden path and spotted Talitha being dragged across the gravel. They exchanged glances and braced themselves.

'About time,' Jeanne said when she saw them. 'It's never good to be late to an interview.'

'Talitha!' Marie screamed.

'Don't worry, she's still breathing,' Jeanne said. 'Though, she won't be after she's executed for killing my brother and his bodyguard. And for releasing the Cockatrice.'

'But she didn-' Marie mumbled as she clocked Jeanne's charges in her head. 'This is all your doing. I bet you even murdered the local priest as well. What did he do to you? Did he suspect you?'

Jeanne shrugged her shoulders. Her indifference as good as a confession.

'Batel-' Jeanne focused on what she deemed important. 'Come work for me. Talented magicians are at a premium and, well, you're wasted pursuing monsters.' She extended her hand of friendship. Money had a set value, but the skills in her employees proved more valuable. 'A court magician for one of the most powerful families in the land has many perks. Your skills deserve proper application.'

'Is that a serious offer?' Batel played his response straight.

Marie widened her eyes. She knew the signs. *This isn't going to be pretty.*

But Jeanne smiled. *Everyone has a price.* 'It is indeed a serious offer.'

Batel started to laugh. It was as if something inside him snapped.

'There's a truth I don't want to believe,' he rasped. 'Idiots pollute the world around them, blinded by greed or ambition and harming those caught in the crossfire. My heart wants this axiom to be a lie.

But, you, you've just reinforced that truth.' He pointed the spike of his halberd towards Jeanne.

Jeanne growled fiercely.

'You think this is amusing? I'm offering you riches most would kill for. But, here you are, even more righteous than Arcana's cleric.'

Marie winced. *That was unnecessary.*

Jeanne refused to be upstaged in her own garden. One by one, she ignited her fingers. 'Your philosophical pretentions bore me. You think you're better than me? Look what I've wrought!'

'You bought a Cockatrice to kill your father because poison was too simple,' Batel scoffed. 'And disposed of your siblings all for consolidation of a power you already owned.' He shook his head dismissively. 'It would be funny if it wasn't so pathetic and people hadn't died.'

'Batel?' Marie was getting frightened by Jeanne's escalating fury; more and more tongues of fire were licking around her fingers and the flames were growing.

Jeanne found his opposition puzzling and insulting.

'Why do you despise me so?'

Batel baulked.

'There's a fool lying in bed after the Cockatrice you brought to your own lands nearly killed him. We swore to protect people from monsters; the man-made ones and their controllers.'

Jeanne hated that he rejected her offer.

'In that case,' she said, 'I'll burn you away along with your ideals.'

She flung the fire, each tongue zooming through the air as bullets.

Marie's staff was already strategically positioned, the flowing Sangterre inside the orb glowed and when she released it, she created a magical barrier, semi-translucent with a whitish hue, in front of Batel and Marie. The fire bounced off the shield without making as much as a mark.

The fires then cooled, snuffed out by the cold air.

Jeanne breathed an irritated sigh.

'I'm going to have exert myself. You'll pay for that.'

Wave after wave of fire crashed into the barrier – pummelling it, melting it, forcing it to crack and splinter.

'She's got some serious firepower,' Marie muttered through clenched teeth. 'She must be using a lot of magic. She surely can't sustain this?'

'Indeed,' Batel grunted. 'It's a test of patience.'

In a break between waves of flames, Marie staked the ground with her staff. A blinding flashing light irradiated from the staff's orb. Jeanne was forced to cover her eyes with her forearm. She could not look directly at the source of light. *Of course, the light of the saintly cleric shines brightly. I need to extinguish it.*

The light faded away giving time for both sides to breathe.

'Not going to cast any spells?' Jeanne provoked. 'Don't you think I'm worthy of your attention?'

'I'm not your father,' Batel snapped back.

Marie saw something snap in Jeanne's eyes. *That was a mistake.*

Jeanne held out her hands, her palms open, and summoned a ball of magical energy. She flung them at Batel's feet where they transformed into bindings that wrapped around his ankles before descending into the ground and securing him to the spot.

What? Batel couldn't lift his feet. His legs were useless. He tried stabbing the bindings with the halberd's spike but he couldn't pierce them. Desperate, he tried sawing at them with the axe-head, but it was no use. He growled. *These ties are too dense. I can't cut through them.*

'So sorry to imprison you, my dear,' Jeanne spat. She focused hard on her hand. A giant crimson fireball began to grow, expanding, swelling, intensifying as she poured more and more of her magic into this blast. Embers fell from its shell to the ground. 'If you refuse to cast any spells then I'll rend you from existence. I'm going to mount your halberd over my fireplace.'

Fire gushed forth.

It slammed into Marie's barrier and maintained relentless pace. Jeanne did not care how much of her magic was poured into this attack. If it drained her, it did not matter as long as she was victorious. Batel and Marie were her final obstacles before her plan could be considered a complete success. Marie fell forward onto one knee, blood flowing from her nose. The barrier began to blister and crack. 'Batel! I, I can't hold ... on.'

Batel shifted his hold on the halberd; now he was grabbing it near its top. With a finger, he stroked the axe-head to bring the magic alive. The metal glowed a luminescent lilac. *Time to play my hand.* He slashed it horizontally, unleashing stored magic. The cut forced the air through the barrier.

It met the fire.

The inferno vanished.

Jeanne staggered backwards, exhausted. She tried clicking her fingers to ignite more fire but nothing happened. *Not good. I've burnt through my magic.* 'Where did my fire go?'

Batel pointed upwards towards the sky.

Jeanne looked up at the clouds.

Above her head, she saw a small ripple. The sky tore open.

Her eyes glowed with the orange radiance of her flames.

She was showered on by her own inferno. With no magic left to defend herself, she fell onto one knee, her arms outstretched to the sides in a gesture of supplication. Then, her silhouette vanished – she was incinerated by her own attack.

The bindings holding Batel and Talitha vanished. Both fell forward. Talitha hit the ground with force, but Batel managed to brace himself for impact. Eyes strained, head pounding, heavy of breath, he lay down next to Talitha and recomposed his equilibrium. *This is why I don't like making giant portals.*

Marie rushed over to them. First, she tended to Talitha, who was slowly coming around.

'Wha- What?' Her hand went to her head. 'What happened?' She looked up, her eyes barely able to focus, and saw she was in Marie's arms. 'You saved me?'

'We're all in this together,' Marie said as she gently raised Talitha to her feet. 'Besides, who else is going to irritate me on an hourly basis?'

Talitha was touched by the implied affection. 'Only hourly?' They both smiled. The status quo resumed.

Then Talitha remembered why she fell.

'But what happened to Lady Jeanne?'

'She's dead. Batel saw to that,' Marie said with a nod towards the magician. *You waited until the last minute to attack. She never saw it coming.*

Batel was lying flat on his back now looking skywards. Drained of magic, he needed to eat and rest. Gently, he got back onto his feet, though his balance was unsteady. *I'm going to sleep this off the way I would a bad hangover.*

Talitha rushed over and embraced him tightly. 'Thank you! Thank you!'

Batel forced a smile. *Well, at least the overexertion was worth it.*

'She was a psycho,' Talitha cried. 'But I stayed strong.' She paused; reconsidered, then beat Batel's chest. 'Never! Ever! Put me in a position like that again!'

'I won't,' Batel promised.

Marie looked around in case any guards were present. From the distance, she heard voices. 'Come on, we need to leave – now!'

Batel picked up his halberd and leant into it.

'After you,' he said.

Talitha put a hand on his arm.

'We can deal with the Cockatrice tomorrow,' she said. 'It's not like it's going to attack Licorne this very minute, is it?'

9 – Le Dieu Parmi les Poulets

Late Afternoon, Licorne

Poulette strolled into the middle of town with her rooster at her side. None of the townspeople paid them attention, after all, they were only chickens. Together they leapt up onto an empty cart and surveyed the village.

The rooster crowed like a trumpet announcing war.

The townspeople laughed thinking it odd that a rooster should crow in the middle of the day. The small children pulled at their mothers' legs wanting to go and play with the chickens.

Then, a second roar bellowed and the Cockatrice strode into the village accompanied by its flock of followers; the zealous chickens all cackling triumphantly.

The locals huddled together in small family-blocks.

The Telliers' guards formed a line between the Cockatrice and the humans; their blue and gold uniforms made them easy targets. They pointed their spears at the Cockatrice and held their positions.

All they had to do was keep their line and not flinch.

Hopefully, the creature would turn around and leave without a fight.

A minute ticked by.

No one moved.

The tension was palpable.

Then, one solider broke rank and threw his spear which travelled silently through the air and pierced the Cockatrice's chest.

The Cockatrice recoiled. It hissed.

The guards needed to keep their discipline now and no one had to die.

Something within the Cockatrice's tortured mind broke. With its claw, it grabbed the spear and pulled it out with little effort.

It snapped the wooden shaft in two.

The guards recoiled in unison, the line still straight though a few inches further back. What they saw amazed them. The open wound on the Cockatrice's chest quickly closed; only an area of dried blood remained.

The Cockatrice leapt on the guard who dared to throw the spear. It placed one claw on his shoulder and with the other clamped his forearm in a grip from which there was no escape. With a single pull, it ripped the whole arm clean off. Strands of muscles flailed as blood gushed out uncontrollably.

The guard cried out in agony.

People scattered in fear.

The Cockatrice turned to the other guards, who had huddled together into a group for protection.

They shivered and shook.

The Cockatrice took its time.

Its beak tore flesh clean off thigh bones.

Its claws sliced upon the breast.

It peeled off the unwanted skin.

It feasted on the livers and human hearts.

All whilst its chicken apostles serenaded it with a verse of vindictive chicken song.

All the guards were dead and the Cockatrice remained hungry, wanting more. It marched deeper into Licorne eager for more delicious treats.

The Galloping Unicorn - Licorne

Watched by the others, Batel placed the vial back on the table in his bedroom. The herbal elixir concocted by Marie entered his system with a jolt. Already, he felt better. *I've regained a small amount of magic.* He tensed his fingers to test them out. *Maybe I have enough to conjure up a medium-sized portal.* He was about to say as such when from somewhere outside screams of terror rippled in through the open windows and doors of the tavern.

There was an exchange of glances.

'That's not good,' said Marie.

Johan looked across at Batel.

'I hardly dare think what's going on,' he said.

Talitha thought she knew.

'What do we do?'

All four rushed out of their room and down the stairs to the street. A rush of people fled by them, some tripping, others pushing in their desperation to get away. They looked down the street to see what they were running away from. And then there it was, in all its bizarre ignoble glory – the Cockatrice.

The creature spotted Johan and stopped in its ravaging tracks. It hissed. It wanted his blood.

Its chicken flock started to cluck, their volume rising menacingly.

Johan pulled out his swords. 'I tried carving you up last time we met! Now I finish the job! Here I come!' He threw himself forward. But the Cockatrice was ready for him. As Johan swung his sword, it ducked its neck out of the way and then leapt forward. Its rooster's beak struck the giant's chest. He bent double in pain, off guard and vulnerable. The Cockatrice's frilled wing then slammed into him, sending him flying backwards, and he landed hard on the ground. 'Ouch!'

Talitha began to panic. 'What's it doing here?'

'Not now!' Batel snapped. 'I'm trying to think of a strategy.'

To the rising, collective clucking of his flock, the Cockatrice advanced slowly, enjoying the moment – playing with its food.

Johan's heart tried to break through his ribcage. *Is this really how I die? To a chorus of singing chickens?*

From behind them, a burst of magical energy surged over Batel's and Marie's heads. It divided into strings of light; bindings latched around the Cockatrice's feet then dug themselves into the ground. The Cockatrice tried raising its feet but couldn't break free. The bindings were keeping it in place. It let out a frustrated bellow that reverberated around the streets.

'Who did that?' Johan asked as he staggered to his feet.

With her black hood billowing, a figure rushed towards them.

'Lady Odette?' Marie cried out in surprise. 'This was your doing?' *If I survive this, I'm going to learn this spell.*

'It's a family trick,' Odette explained, trying her best to keep her focus where it mattered – in keeping those bindings in place. Clearly not as strong as Jeanne, her determination to save Licorne was nevertheless clear.

Marie acknowledged her resolve. *Right.*

Talitha mobilised. She sprinted behind the Cockatrice's position.

'You coward!' Odette cried out.

Batel, however, raised his hand.

'Just watch.'

Talitha pointed her knives at the choir of chickens to silence them, then mounted the Cockatrice's back and stabbed it with both her knives simultaneously. The Cockatrice reared against its bindings and roared in pain, its frilled wings tense and rigid, and although it tried to shake her off, its body movements became random and jerky. Talitha clutched the handles of her enchanted daggers and let out a wild scream.

Her daggers started to glow white. *What's going on? What's activated its enchantment?*

Something was pushing against the daggers. *What? No way?* The Cockatrice's magical defences were reacting to a foreign attack. It rejected the daggers. The Cockatrice's magic pushed the knives out of the wounds.

Muscles healed.

Wounds disappeared.

The daggers ceased to be anchors for her. She fell backwards and bounced off the Cockatrice's tail to land awkwardly on the ground; the reaction force of the earth punishing her for her bravery.

The daggers fell on top of her. Their expulsion from the Cockatrice complete. Its flock of poultry swarmed her, pecking at her, picking up her arms and swinging them about. Talitha knocked away as many of the hens and roosters trying to break her skin as she could. Poulette tried to attack her leg. Talitha kicked her away and she flew through the air, spinning on an invisible spit, her pained cry satisfying to Talitha's ears.

She managed to get to her feet.

I am not chicken feed!

She picked up her daggers and dashed to safety before the Cockatrice's tail could swipe her away. *It can expel our weapons then heal. How are we going to kill this thing?*

But the Cockatrice made no attempt to attack her. Another prey had presented itself.

Batel had already begun his charge forth and drove his halberd forward. Its spike penetrated the captive Cockatrice's chest, piercing the flesh and cutting through its scales. The Cockatrice roared in pain. But once again its magical defences activated and it pushed the halberd spear out of its body.

Batel's eyes widened. *Not good!*

He withdrew his halberd before the Cockatrice could grab it and snap it in half. For his troubles, he was swatted away like a fly by the Cockatrice's neck which generated enough force for the impact to feel as hard as crashing into granite. Coughing, spluttering blood, Batel looked up at his opponent.

The Cockatrice exerted its might. The binds that chained it to the earth shattered and the magical energies returned to the ground.

This can't be happening!

Batel, struggling to get to his feet, was now within clawing range.

Marie staked her staff into the ground. A barrier was projected. It blocked the Cockatrice from disembowelling Batel or Johan, who was now running to his friend's side. The creature clawed angrily at the barrier. The magical shield bent from the impact. Johan picked up Batel and placed him on his feet. He stood winded.

'Don't fight it head on.' Johan spoke from experience.

Batel coughed and wheezed. 'Lesson learnt.'

He staggered back to the protection of Marie, Odette and Talitha just as the Cockatrice's beak shattered the barrier. Shards of magical energy fell like glass and were absorbed back into the earth when they touched the soil.

Johan was the first line of the defence with his two blades.

'I'm not finished yet!' he shouted. His battle cry was met by the bone-shattering force of a crack of the Cockatrice's tail and he was sent crashing through the wall of the Galloping Unicorn. He got up slowly, winded, and wiped away the dust and debris. Heavily, he rejoined the allies.

All were bloodied and beaten.

They were the last line of defence; all other townspeople had been killed or had fled. If the Cockatrice killed them; it claimed the town.

The Cockatrice drew near.

Its footsteps sounded like slow, deliberate drumbeats. The lowering pitch of its chicken followers' songs thickened the air. The gruesome reality set in; in a few moments, they could be ripped apart limb from limb by the most appalling of creatures that ever dared grace the world's stage and the last thing that their mortal eyes would see would be a rooster's beak gouging out their hearts.

'We're not going to be able to kill this thing!' Talitha cried in mortal terror.

Odette stared blankly at the monster in front of her.

'What did you buy, Jeanne?' she cried out, not wanting to be third Tellier to be slain that day.

'BATEL!' Marie shouted. Johan, Talitha and Odette joined in. 'BATEL, do something!'

The magician growled; the pressure stifling his ability to think. His mettle was being tested. *What do I do? If I can't kill this monster then we're all going to die.*

His mind clicked into action. *Hold on! The Cockatrice expels foreign objects first before it starts to heal. Johan and Talitha might not possess enough magic to keep their weapons embedded, but I might be able to do so with some prior damage. I just need a clear shot.*

'Lady Odette! Bind its legs!' he commanded with all his heart.

'Right!' Odette didn't question. She rubbed her hands together to generate the magical bindings and threw them at the creature. They wrapped around the Cockatrice's feet and clamped them tightly together before burrowing into the ground and securing the beast.

The Cockatrice screeched; fought back.

'Stab it in the neck!' Batel pointed his halberd to the place where the rooster and serpent sections joined. Before the Cockatrice had chance to exert its strength and break the binds, Talitha and Johan leapt on opposite sides of its neck and stabbed hard – Talitha drilled in both daggers and Johan speared the Cockatrice's flesh with his sword.

The creature roared in agony and swung its neck to the side. Its head slammed into Johan and floored him.

Why always me?

His sword remained embedded but it glowed as it reacted to the Cockatrice's magical defences that were pushing it out of the wound.

Talitha took evasive action, pulled out her daggers and took to the ground immediately to avoid any chance of being swatted away by its tail.

Batel ran his fingers over the halberd's axe head to enchant it. It glowed its mysterious lilac glow. *If I can get a clean shot, then my magic will set up a competition with the Cockatrice's magic. If I'm lucky, trying to expel my halberd with disrupt its healing.* 'Marie! Blind it!'

The bedazzling beacon shone brightly from Marie's staff.

The Cockatrice closed its eyes, backstepped and flinched. Batel charged in, both hands on the shaft of his halberd. With all his power, he swung his weapon. The halberd's axe-head dug into the wound that Johan's sword made in the Cockatrice's neck. As the first blade fell to the ground, redundant, the halberd cut deeper into the fresh wound and the Cockatrice's magical defences tried to push the weapon out. Two mystical forces waged war.

Batel continued forward. He knew what he needed to do.

A final burst of magic created a safe portal for his axe-head to travel through which bypassed the Cockatrice's defences.

The cut could not be stopped. No healing could take place.

The Cockatrice's head rolled away.

The monster was dead.

Chicken blood showered upon Batel's face and robes. His legs gave way. He fell to the ground exhausted. *I did it!*

The chicken zealots paused.

They looked at each other; they had lost their cult leader, their saviour. There was an uneasy quiet. All the humans looked at each other wondering what retribution would rain down upon them for murdering the poultry deity, but the chickens scattered, madly clucking. Some ran into each other. Poulette lead the evacuation.

Peace returned to Licorne.

Batel beheld the fallen beast as blood dripped from the halberd's axe-head. *One less abomination for the world to worry about.* Within himself, he felt calmly serene. He'd reached a new equilibrium. He looked back at his allies. *For those who want to sow madness, there are also those who want to restore a semblance of order. With these people, I can help rid the world of these engineered abominations.*

10 – La Nouvelle Commande Tellier

Tellier Mansion – Licorne

Odette stood beneath her father's towering portraits as the only remaining Tellier. The chairs where Henri and Jeanne sat before were empty and the weight of responsibility fell heavily on her shoulders. In her hands, bags of gold coins.

'So that should settle all rewards,' she said as she handed them over to her five heroes.

'We shall feast merrily,' said Johan, who was so happy he almost broke into one of his drinking songs before the drinking had even begun.

Talitha smiled but kept what she was planning to do with her share of the gold close to her heart. *My investments are my own business.*

Matto saw his bag of gold was fuller than those given to others and guessed Odette was as generous with her compensation as she had been with her slaps, but the reward felt hollow. *This wasn't my victory. I've proved Batel he was right. I was a fool. I can't bear the shame.*

Odette turned her attention to Marie.

'Pass me your staff,' she instructed.

Marie did as she asked.

Odette stroked the orb, the Sangterre inside responded to her touch and glowed. Eyes closed, focus absolute, she recited a chant under her breath. The Sangterre stopped shining. She passed back the staff. 'There. The binding spell is contained inside. But be warned, you'll need to practice. As a skill, it will take a while to perfect.'

Marie bowed her head in thanks.

Appreciative, Odette smiled.

Finally, she turned to Batel and handed over the purchase order for the Cockatrice. She could not give it away any quicker. 'Get that paper out of my manor.'

Batel accepted it. It had been redacted, of course, but it was a clue to the creature's provenance and that was all that mattered.

'What will you do now, Lady Odette?' Marie asked.

'My first order was a ban on killing chickens,' Odette informed them. 'I don't want my legacy to be tainted by a chicken massacre nor do I want Licorne to become the centre for a great poultry crusade.'

Everyone laughed.

The tension of the past few days released.

They all knew Odette didn't know what was going to happen now, nor had she been groomed to run the family. But fate deals strange hands.

'You're going to be fine,' Marie said; she trusted Odette. 'May Arcana guide you.'

Odette bowed graciously, forever grateful for their assistance.

'Thank you. You are always welcome here.'

All five of them bowed in respect and took their leave.

In the hallway, Cherie smiled and nodded at Marie. In return, Marie gave her a subtle wink. *Your secret is safe with me.*

Gardens – The Tellier Mansion, Licorne

Their adventure in Licorne had come to its conclusion. Although they could revel in their victory, there was bound to be another monster attack somewhere. They paused for a moment in the mansion's gardens before returning to the dangers of the world outside.

Matto stood at a distance from the group, the unwanted fifth member. He clutched his bag of gold tightly.

'It's time I was on my way,' he said.

The others looked to Batel, who remained silent. Matto braced himself.

'Have a good journey home, Matto,' Batel said. 'It is best if you go. You're not cut out for this. You'd be a fool to continue.'

'This fool,' Matto said, 'is on his own journey.'

And with that, he left.

'What was that about?' Talitha asked as soon as he was out of earshot.

'Wounded pride,' Johan presumed.

Batel pursed his lips. *Let's hope it is just that.* He held up the purchase slip for the Cockatrice.

'Well done,' he said. 'We now have a clue.' Though the name of Jeanne Tellier and the address of the Telliers had been redacted, the crucial information was still present. 'The Cockatrice was imported. It was bought in the western port city of Sirene under the company name *Arcana's Shadow.*'

Marie could not let this insult go unpunished. *Heretics! How dare they use Arcana's name in vain?* 'Is that where we're heading then, Sirene?'.

'Not tonight,' Johan insisted; he planned to feast and celebrate their achievements. 'We shall make this night a night to be remembered for generations. Songs will be sung about our victories.'

'You've already been doing that for six days,' Talitha objected. 'This village is getting bored of you.'

'Nonsense. Leave the party at its height!'

Marie sought some clarity and sensibility to his proceedings.

'Batel?'

Batel looked at the bronze statue of the unicorn that now adorned the garden. *You'll outlast all of us. You'll be standing here for future generations to come gather and speculate about your legend.* He held on tightly to the purchase order in one hand, his halberd in the other. *I wonder what legacy I'll leave behind.* He looked at his allies and affirmed his resolve to himself.

'Come on, let's go.'

They all left to return for Licorne for one final night. Talitha remained a few steps behind scribbling in her notebook. With her quill, she carefully finished the last sentence in her bestiary and made the full stop pronounced.

And so ends the tale of the Tellier Cockatrice.

The Gulliver's Gryphon

Arcana's Bestiary Page 2

Magic, like any other resource, will always have mankind dreaming of how to exploit it. There are always individuals who seek to such resources to advance their own ends. Not even the borders between countries are an effective barrier for such greed and ambition. And when the promise of grand riches is at stake, suddenly a monster seems a reasonable investment to protect such fortunes ... until something goes wrong that is ...

1 – L'Offre du Seigneur

Nightfall – Sirene Dock

La Mer Étroite is still tonight. Too still.

Batel stood at the water's edge and licked the salt from his lips. His purple robes caught in the sea breeze and he shivered from the cooling air filling out his sleeves. *I've never been a sea person. There's too much hiding beneath the waves.* Scrunched in his hand, a piece of parchment delivered by a carrier pigeon which had inauspiciously landed on his enchanted halberd's spike earlier that afternoon; the penmanship was calligraphic, or at least it attempted to be – Batel's eyes caught the erratic pen strokes. *Someone's acting above their position.* The message read:

I have a job for your magician. Come meet me at the docks overlooking the Mercian Channel at nightfall.

Gulliver.

Mercian Channel? The Mercians, who lived on the other side of the channel, had a habit on stamping their name on lands and bodies of water that were shared rather than owned; he knew the stretch of water as 'La Mer Étroite'. Batel's suspicions were matched by his curiosity. *I've only been in Sirene for a day and I already have a job offer. News from Licorne travels fast but it should not have travelled across the channel. Whoever this Gulliver is, I'm suspicious of him.*

Something in the sea air gnawed at him.

This whole town sleeps with fear. As a warning, the enchanted silver axe-head at the top of his halberd glowed a faint lilac; Batel was wary of an ambush. He gripped the Sangterre-treated oak pole tightly, ready to swing his halberd the moment danger showed itself; the runes etched on the axe-head were ready to express his magic. *I have enemies here. I'm sure I've been spotted by agents of Arcana's Shadow. I don't like being summoned into the open but I need to draw out those residing in the gloom.*

'You received my message, magician,' a male voice called out, his tongue catching on the final word.

Batel noted the resentment and took a moment before turning to face his summoner. *And he's already disappointed me.* Calmly, Batel turned and analysed the approaching stranger's demeanour. *I see he's from Etellia not Mercia, but he's trying hard to mask it. Or has he been at sea too long?*

A sea captain, his cheeks scarred and skin taut, appeared out of the night air. He wore a black leather jacket that did not sit well on his shoulders – it was as if it was not his to wear. Clearly, he was not a navy man or an officer of any legitimate shipping enterprise. Instead, he wore the aura of a smuggler with pride of infamy and rule breaking.

Batel accepted the reality of the man standing in front of him. *I know my companions won't approve of me dealing with him but I accepted long ago that stopping Arcana's Shadow will require getting my hands dirty.* 'You must be Gulliver?'

'I admit I wasn't expecting the halberd. Magicians usually carry wands ... and wands snap easily.'

Gulliver glided past Batel and then stopped at the dock's edge to stare out into the calm sea. Being confined to land was proving intolerable to his seafarer's heart – he was itchy, jumpy, constantly on edge. *I miss the rocking of my boat. I miss the thrill of the chase. Soon I'll be back on the sweet smooth waves.*

Batel could not avoid the distain in Gulliver's voice. *He's not even giving me eye contact. He hates magicians. But he's not the most well-guarded of people. Maybe I can use that to my advantage.* 'La Mer

Étroite can be treacherous at the best of times. It must be important for you to return home to Mercia.'

'I recognise no country as my home. The sea is my true home. I have not come ashore for pleasure.' Gulliver turned to face Batel but only to sneer. *He's no peasant magician. He clearly comes from a wealthy family.* 'I heard an arrogant magician killed a Cockatrice.' He turned back to face his beloved ocean again and Batel saw him picking away at his long, dirty nails.

'And why do you need an arrogant magician's help?'

Gulliver wanted to throttle Batel but stopped himself. Dismemberment by halberd would be counterproductive. *You're lucky you're useful otherwise I'd dump you out at sea.* 'I need you to kill a Gryphon.'

Batel caught his breath. *A gryphon? Are they manufacturing Gryphons now?*

Gulliver revelled in the glow of Batel's horror. *Not so cocky now, are you?* 'That's right. A Gryphon.'

'There's a Gryphon near Sirene! Why? How?'

Gulliver kicked at the ground. 'I bought it here.'

'You did what? Why? Why would do that?' Batel slammed his halberd into the salt-rich wooden planks. *This idiot has single-handily endangered everyone.*

'I tasked it to guard a treasure, the vast riches of a Mercian Lord, and I've come to reclaim that treasure, but the stupid beast disobeys me. It needs to die. I'll pay you handsomely.' Gulliver provided the proposed details of the transaction.

Batel growled. *Stay calm. Think. Gulliver might have information about Arcana's Shadow and their import operations. If I can trick him, he'll have to surrender what he knows.* 'I accept.' Gulliver raised an eyebrow in surprise. He had not expected this to be so easy. Batel continued. 'But you must be patient. These beasts are not easy to kill.'

'You have twenty-four hours.' Gulliver imposed a strict deadline.

Batel winced. *That's tight.* 'What happens then?'

'Don't disappoint me, magician ... or you'll find out.'

Gulliver departed, a smile tugging at his lips.

Batel rolled his eyes. *Part of Gulliver is desperate for my help. The other part would love me to fail.*

Alone now, he filled his lungs with the ocean air. *If I can find out who is bringing these monsters into the country, it will be worth enduring Gulliver's prejudices. He won't hesitate to stab me in the back if given the chance.* Batel looked up at the starry sky and beheld the waning moon. Something caught in the back of his throat. *A smuggler lying should be my default assumption. These professional criminals are tougher to deal with than treacherous nobility. They've been raised to lie to survive not as a passion project.*

Batel allowed himself a small smile. *Having said that, I know two of my companions will be dreaming of the potential bounty. It seems we've found ourselves another engineered abomination.*

2 – La Flèche de L'Archer

The Humming Mermaid – Sirene Town Centre

The three companions waited silently in the bar of The Humming Mermaid for Batel to return.

Seated at the table in the corner, Marie glowered at all the tacky mermaid merchandise; Sirene was as obsessed with mermaids as Licorne was with unicorns, but here admiration had segued into an unhealthy fixation. She was in a foul mood anyway, the last thing she needed was to spend her evening surrounded by a load of drunken idiots lusting over fictional woman – topless fictional woman with fish tails. Batel *could at least have had the courtesy of telling us where he was going; he's developing a nasty habit of not telling us until he gets back.*

She glanced around the bar and noticed people staring at her; she stood out in these tawdry surroundings; after all, a blond religious cleric wearing saintly white robes with ribbons flowing from the sleeves does not normally frequent such surroundings. Next to her, her wooden staff rested against the wall and the silvery, viscous Sangterre in its orb glistened and tumbled. It could detect traces of magic and relay them to her, giving her real-time information about those residing in this town. *We were caught off guard in Licorne. We can't afford for the same to happen here.*

'Another!' Johan, sitting opposite her, slammed his tankard on the table. The giant had drunk his daily quota of ale and a haze was starting to fall over his decision-making abilities. His muscles pushed against his segmented body armour, sticky from all the spilt beer; his unkept beard and numerous facial scars repelled any unwanted advances towards the group. He was spellbound by the picture of a red-haired mermaid. 'Half-woman, half-fish-'

'Sounds like you fancy her?' Talitha, who was sitting next to Marie, sniped as she scribbled on the back page of her bestiary with her enchanted quill – her tied-back hazelnut hair jumped every time she had a new thought. Taking notes at the back allowed her to preserve the front pages for her detailed entries. 'A mermaid lover sounds like a slippery affair.'

'I would never take one as a lover,' Johan decreed with a confidence and clarity of thought that surprised both Marie and Talitha.

'You have clearly thought about this,' Talitha snapped.

Johan took the cue and shut up. Marie blocked him from her vision with her hand. *I wish I didn't know you.*

Talitha returned to her notebook and buried her face into its pages. *I guess it's been a while since a woman paid him attention.* 'Loneliness is a cruel mistress, Johan.'

He let out a hoot of laughter.

'No, you misunderstand! I would wrestle these mistresses of the sea to reclaim the waters from their siren grasp!'

He hiccupped, then belched.

Talitha frantically waved her hand in front of her nose to dispel the foul, malty breath. 'That's disgusting!'

Johan ignored her and continued. 'A lover would try to out-wrestle me! That's why mermaids would make terrible lovers – they're too slippery!'

'Marie!' Talitha whinged. 'Do something to stop him.'

But Marie was distracted. Her eyes were drawn to her staff; something had caught its attention. The Sangterre in the orb thickened and tumbled more quickly. *Someone nearby is using magic.* She glanced around the tavern and caught sight of a man sitting in the convenient shadows of the corner, ostensibly minding his own business. He was writing in a hefty, foolscap, hard-bound book that appeared to be a ledger of some sort. His hand moved first across the page and then ran down to enter what she assumed were numbers at the bottoms of columns. People moved around him as if he were not there. Marie shivered; goosebumps fortified her skin. *He's casting a perception-altering spell. He's not invisible. Just inconspicuous. Who is he?*

The man looked up and Marie jerked her head away. *I hope he didn't notice me.* A moment later, the man returned to his writings and she breathed a sigh of relief. *That was close. I need to let Batel know about this when he gets back.*

'MARIE!' Talitha screeched again.

Marie snapped back into her colleagues' pointless banter. 'Keep annoying her, Johan.'

Talitha puffed out her cheeks. 'Such a helpful cleric.'

'Will you be quiet!' Marie's focus was on the mysterious figure rather than Talitha's habitual squabbling. 'No-one wants to hear a child scream.'

'And no-one wants to listen to an old hag!' Talitha was not letting go; she was met with a bonk to the head from Marie's staff.

'So old,' she whispered as she felt for a dent in her skull. Nothing. She leant over and flicked through Marie's long blond tresses with the end of her forefinger. 'Is that a grey hair?'

Marie grabbed at the offending strand and drew it in front of her eyes.

Talitha laughed without mercy nor kindness. *I win.*

Marie realised she had been duped and hit Talitha with her staff again. 'Don't joke about that!'

Johan shook his head at them. 'You two are cruel to each other.'

'JOHAN!!' called a gruff voice. All three turned to see a giant of a man who matched Johan's size and bulk, his face bearing the scars of many a fight. People scurried to the corners of the room like mice as he made his way across the bar.

'HENRIK?' Johan rasped. He rose to his feet and his face hardened ready for a messy fight. He rolled up his sleeves and cracked his knuckles.

'Johan! No!' Marie and Talitha tried to stop him by pulling at his sleeves, but he yanked his arms free with little effort and stomped towards Henrik.

Johan and Henrik squared up to each other, noses touching. Boos were volleyed at Henrik – a traveller who had already made himself an enemy of Sirene by beating up some of the locals to make his mark. But tonight was different; tonight was personal – the latest round of a feud spanning years.

Marie tightened her grip on her staff, Sangterre churning in its orb. *I'll have to restrain them.*

Both men puffed out their chests and felt the other's heavy breath fall onto their face as both simultaneously threw a punch across the other's jaw. Blood and spit flew from their mouths, their necks ricocheting to the side. They licked the blood from their lips and wiped their chins.

'You still punch weak,' Henrik taunted. Johan snarled and squared up for round two, both combatants waiting until the other blinked.

Something flew in front of their eyes. Their hearts jumped as an arrow flew through the narrow space between them and dug into the wall on the far side of them.

As one, they turned to the source of the missile and saw a young, female archer with wild, braided hair that fell to her waist. Already reloading her bow, she glared at them with an irritated scowl carved upon her handsome face.

Marie loosened her grip on her staff. *It seems I'm not needed.*

The gathered crowd fell silent; they recognised her authority. Talitha noticed she was wearing a beast's fur around her neck. A trophy. *She's a hunter.*

The archer now aimed the bow at Henrik; her previous shot was a warning. 'Scram!'

Henrik took the measure of the room; it was not on his side.

'I could snap you like a twig, Carla,' he grumbled, but it was not his habit to fight those he lacked a grudge against, not unless he was being paid to cave skulls in. He shrugged off the disappointment of another scrap with an old adversary and walked, head held high, towards the exit. He was the biggest threat in room and he knew it.

At that moment, Batel opened the door. Henrik stopped before the magician and, from his giant height, looked down at him.

Batel reeled from this unwanted surprise. *Henrik? What's he doing here?*

As if to answer his question, Henrik spat on his right shoe. The collected gathering gasped at his audacity, his rudeness. No-one disrespected a magician, especially if they did not possess the magic with which to retaliate.

Batel looked down at the unpleasant drool. He rubbed his fingers across the axe-head on his halberd and it stared to glow a faint lilac. Carla's brow furrowed. *It's enchanted?*

The crowd gasped again and retreated to the far wall, leaving Carla, Marie, Johan and Talitha to stand alone at the front. Batel glared directly into Henrik's eye and smirked. He was not going to be intimidated. 'The other shoe, please.'

Henrik growled. *You've not changed at all.*

Carla's eyes widened. *Is he brave? Is he stupid? Henrik could snap him in two.*

But Henrik barged through the doorway and departed without another word. Batel allowed himself a smile, but an unwelcome thought niggled. *What are the chances that he's Gulliver's hired muscle?* His thought was short-lived. Cheers from the patrons distracted him. *OK? What did I miss?*

'Alright, people! Show's over!' Carla cried out. The crowd moaned but dispersed and the patrons returned to their drinking. This would be their fuel for conversations for the next three weeks.

Meanwhile, Marie dashed over to Batel, sighing in relief. 'Never a dull moment with you.'

Batel smiled but had other concerns; he noticed Johan massaging his jaw. *Johan and Henrik always fought.*

'Who was he?' asked Talitha, who guessed the others already knew him from adventures they had together before she joined their group. 'That seemed personal.'

'It involves betrayal, poor life choices and Henrik being left for dead in a pig sty,' Batel said with a sideways glance at Johan. But he was mentioning no names because, for now, he was more concerned about the present. 'I hate to mention this at a delicate time-' The group looked to him, expectant. 'But we've got another monster to kill.'

Marie's face dropped; she dreaded the permutations. She covered her mouth with her fingertips. *Oh no!*

Talitha, meanwhile, squealed with excitement. *I can write another page in my bestiary.*

'STOP IT! STOP BEING EXCITED!' Marie bonked Talitha on the head with her staff.

Carla ignored them and strolled over, eager to inspect Batel closer. *Never seen a magician with a halberd before. Wonder why he doesn't use a wand.* 'You handled that thug well,' she said, sidling towards him.

Marie did not take kindly to her familiarity. She dashed over and placed herself in front of Batel as a barrier between them. *Stop looking at him like that.* But she could not tell whether Batel even noticed Carla's advances – he appeared to be preoccupied with the arrow in the wall, which he assumed was her doing. *A huntress should have extensive knowledge of the local area.* 'Tell me, archer. Do you know anything about a Gryphon?'

Carla shuddered at the mention of the name and the inn fell oddly silent. All of them were afraid of the beast that plagued their waking thoughts. They could not believe that anyone would seek it out – surely not even magicians would be stupid enough to pursue such a mighty force?

Marie and Talitha stood open-mouthed. *That is what we need to kill?*

Batel turned to the huntress.

'We hunt monsters,' he said, gesturing towards the rest of his group with an open hand. 'If you want us to get rid of yours, then we require your local expertise. Would you mind helping us?' He did not want to assume.

'Yes.' Carla accepted the proposition without a moment's hesitation.

Marie rolled her eyes. *Of course you wouldn't mind.*

Batel signalled Johan to go upstairs for a meeting. The giant complied with a nod and up the stairs he trudged, blood still running out of his mouth. Marie and Talitha followed. Batel let the lilac glow on his halberd fade. *Henrik being here complicates things, but no problem is unsurmountable.* He was about to join the others when he noticed the man sitting in the corner, hiding in the shadows. *What's he doing here?*

The man closed his ledger and made a deliberate effort to make eye contact with Batel. He wanted the magician to notice him and force him to acknowledge his presence before turning in for the night.

Batel grimaced. *If he's here then that complicates matters even more.* Yet, as Batel joined his companions upstairs, he wondered if this shadow-seeker might also, in an unexpected way, serve to simplify matters.

Left in the bar on her own, Carla walked over to the wall and pulled out her arrow. *Maybe my prayers have been answered. The goddess Arcana has provided me with hope that Sirene can be saved from smugglers and monsters. Let's see what this halberd bearer can do.*

3 – Le Plan de la Chasse

Batel's Room – The Humming Mermaid

Batel let the others take their places first, wherever they found most comfortable. He wanted those he led to feel at ease and valued. Johan sat grumpily at the end of the bed staring blankly forward, his blooded chin resting on folded hands. Marie and Talitha brought in chairs from their rooms and placed them in front row positions. Batel was about to begin when there was a knock on the door. The four friends exchanged glances.

'You'd better let her in,' Batel said, knowing before the door was even opened who it was going to be.

Talitha sprang to her feet and dashed to the door.

'Batel said you'd better come in,' she said to Carla with a grin.

Carla nodded her thanks and joined the rest of the group in the room. She took her position leaning against the far wall – an external consultant.

Batel nodded his welcome, then looked around the room, took stock of everyone's positions and noted their choices; considered them significant. He understood everyone's roles and strengths – it was down to him to use those skills for maximum impact.

Carla went straight to business. 'Tell me,' she said. 'How you know about the Gryphon?'

Batel sat in the chair at the front left vacant for him.

'A smuggler named Gulliver hired me to kill it. Do you know him?'

Carla grimaced. Marie, on the other hand, was more vocal in her disapproval.

'You let a criminal hire us? Need I remind you that I am a cleric of Arcana. I have a duty. A status. I cannot be consorting with criminals.'

'Gulliver's desperate,' Batel replied with calming clarity. 'If we play this right, we can get valuable information about our true enemy. To discover the sources of these monsters, we must unfortunately dive into the criminal underworld to find those who swim its sewage.'

'You deal with him. Not me.' Marie drew a line.

'Fine. I will shield you from culpability,' Batel promised.

Carla cracked her knuckles. 'These smugglers are ruining Sirene. This used to be a legitimate port before they settled here. Crime is on the rise and they are deterring boats from docking. They need to go. If killing the Gryphon will rid the place of them, then we have to play them at their own game.'

Johan stared forward at a vacant portion of the stone wall. 'Is Henrik with the smugglers?'

'Yes. He's the worst of all of them.' Carla wanted to spit in disgust.

'A mercenary with no standards,' Johan chuntered.

'How do you know him?' Carla asked.

Batel and Marie glanced at each other. There were things Johan preferred not to discuss about his past. Not even the usually forthright Talitha dared to ask.

Johan stood up. Hearts ticked faster. 'He has no honour.'

He said no more and Talitha and Carla were left to fill the gaps for themselves. *No love lost there.*

Johan coughed and cleared his throat. He scratched his beard. He changed the subject. 'Where's the Gryphon then?'

'There's a cave in the woods outside Sirene.' Carla walked over to the window and pointed to the north-east beyond the line of houses lit by wood fires. She shivered. *Good hunters have died trying to kill that beast.* 'The Gryphon rarely wanders far. It will kill anything that gets too close and eat it – humans included. No matter if we use swords, arrows or spears, it simply heals itself, no problem. It cannot be killed.'

Talitha checked her bestiary and used her finger to follow the path of each line that she had written about her adventures in Licorne. 'Just like the Cockatrice.'

Carla cocked her eyebrow. 'What?'

'It's a half-chicken, half-dragon,' Talitha enthused.

Carla gasped, if not at her enthusiasm then at the thought of the beast itself.

Batel hid a smirk. *At least not everyone knows who we are.* 'A Cockatrice is a monster that possesses similar abilities to the Gryphon you described. Though, if I hazard a guess, I would say the Gryphon is a higher category of beast, a more expensive investment.'

'You've fought against such creatures before?' Carla's worldview was expanding faster than she could keep up with.

'Yes. It was quite an ordeal.' Marie undersold the affair with light laughter.

Carla noticed the faraway look in Batel's eyes. The magician had heard tales of Gryphons. Compared to the Cockatrice, they were nobler beasts which featured more prominently in folklore, their gold-edged images drawn in the margins of medieval manuscripts. *Half-lion. Half-eagle. King of the land and sky.* He blinked himself back to reality. *It would make sense that this particular creature came from Mercia first before being shipped here by Gulliver.*

'I still can't believe one of these creatures actually exists. It sounds unnatural.' Carla shivered and cradled her arms around herself.

'They're manufactured.' Batel continued to pile on the information.

Carla caught her breath. 'Who on earth ... I mean, who would do that?'

Marie gripped her staff. 'Vile blasphemers. They call themselves Arcana's Shadow. We came to Sirene because we suspected this port is the place where the monsters are being imported into Etellia.'

Carla riled. *This is wrong! No-one in Sirene asked for this. How did it happen? Who allowed this to happen?* 'Count me in on your quest.'

'Gulliver has given us a twenty-four-hour deadline,' Batel informed.

'That's not long,' Talitha squawked.

'No. He wants me to fail. He has something planned for us. And given that he's running out of options, I suspect we don't want to find out what it is.'

Johan itched to swing his enchanted blades. He tensed his arm muscles. The glory and prestige of killing a Gryphon was alluring. 'I won't let you fail.'

'Good.' Batel smiled. His eyes shifted to Carla. 'Can I count on you, archer?'

'You can.' Carla was eager to partake in a legendary hunt. *We might have a chance if all of us go together.*

Talitha looked up from her bestiary. She had already created the second page and written 'Gryphon' as the title in the best calligraphy she could. *I'm getting better.* She put down her enchanted quill. 'What do you want me to do?'

Batel gave the matter some thought. *We have three fighters ready to battle the Gryphon. But I also need someone to do some digging into the activities of Arcana's Shadow.* 'Investigate the docks. Do your usual snooping around. Walk through the doors only a thief knows how to. We need something to twist Gulliver's arm. I am sure that someone as resourceful as you can find something.'

Talitha smiled gleefully. 'Will do.' She was eager to do some preparatory work. *Smugglers have treasures. I want to see what I can steal.*

'Batel,' Marie interrupted.

Batel pursed his lips. *Something's spooked her.* He noticed that the Sangterre in the orb of her staff was churning and tumbling in the background. *Her staff has been analysing something. And I can guess what it has spotted.*

'Batel, may I speak with you in my chambers once this meeting is over?' Before he had chance to answer, Marie opened the door and departed, taking her chair with her.

Am I in trouble?

Her abrupt departure left everyone uneasy. Johan and Talitha thought it most unlike her to be secretive and flustered. Carla sensed this was not the usual power dynamic.

'The rest of you, get some sleep,' Batel told them. 'I'll talk to Marie.'

Johan and Talitha took their leave, Talitha taking her chair and her bestiary with her – she intended to plan out the Gryphon's entry carefully and precisely.

Carla, on the other hand, refused to move.

'Is everything alright?' Batel asked as he held open the door and gestured for her to leave.

'You're intriguing , magician. How did you get into hunting monsters for a living? Someone like you could make a handy living brewing potions or advising royalty on the future on their monarchies.'

'Good night,' Batel answered. He signalled her to leave immediately.

She did so with a playful smile. *I'm not done with you yet, halberd boy.*

Once he closed the door behind her, Batel ran his hand through his hair and sighed. *Carla is going to ask questions, isn't she? And I'm not always going to be able to answer.* He took a deep breath. *I need to manage Carla carefully. But she's not my priority right now.*

Marie's Room – The Humming Mermaid

The knock came. It was later than Marie expected it to be. She opened the door to find Batel standing in the hallway looking grim.

'Can I come in?' She nodded imperceptibly and he crossed the threshold into a room where he noted that the mermaid iconography had been put out of sight or turned away from view. *Marie is a cleric of Arcana; she does not tolerate the ridiculous.* 'Do you mind telling me what's on your mind?' he asked.

Marie sat on the bed, her hands fidgeting. She gazed out of the window. 'Remember in Licorne you told me that we operate in both the light and the shadows.'

'Yes,' Batel recalled. *I know where this is going.*

'Did you know when you went to the docks that the person you were going to meet with was a criminal?' She glared at him hard, waiting for an answer.

Batel rested his halberd against the wall. 'No, but I saw an opportunity and I took it.'

'And you did not consult me? ... You brought Talitha along without my approval. You promised she would be reformed but you are making use of her talents – if I can call them that. But to take a job and money from a criminal? How much do the ends justify the means, Batel?'

Batel took a seat on the edge of the bed next to her. He needed to tread with care and delicate precision. He did not speak until Marie had said her piece. She was, in theory, the most respected figure of their group and exuded authority.

'And then there's the archer,' she continued. 'A stranger who swans in and you tell her everything! What next? Who else are you going to recruit without our input?' Marie paused to calm her breathing; it was unbecoming of a cleric of Arcana to be angry. She should always be composed, a moral beacon in the lives of ordinary people. 'Well? Say something.'

Batel remained silent, accepting her points. He was open to criticism. *You can't keep everyone happy all the time.* 'We're close to finding Arcana's Shadow and snuffing them out. I had to act quickly before Gulliver vanished.' He bit the inside of his lip. 'If it makes you feel better, I am disposable in the eyes of the Church of Arcana if things go wrong.'

Marie exhaled for five seconds, resigning herself to the fact that they were going to need each other to achieve their goal of stamping out the monsters infecting Etellia, but all the same he worried her. *You've got a one-track mind, Batel. You'll stop at nothing and don't mind stooping to levels far beneath your standing to achieve your goals. I do trust you, but people are going to get hurt.* Her mind fell onto their enemies. They needed stopping; of that she was in no doubt. She took a deep breath. 'Something in Sirene disturbs me.'

'How so?'

'There was someone sitting in the bar tonight. He was casting a perception-altering spell so no-one noticed him. That kind of magic worries me. It's not forbidden per se but it raises questions.'

'Indeed?' Batel pretended not to have seen him.

'He was writing in a ledger. He looked like a salesman. I have no evidence to say why but I think he belongs to Arcana's Shadow. There's something ... tainted about him.'

She's not wrong. 'It's possible. The magic you describe is subtle and discreet. I imagine most magicians would not be able to see through it. You may have stumbled onto a lead.'

He smiled at her and she pretended not to notice. *There, he does it again. I get angry and frustrated, then he smiles and I feel better.* She shook her head in dismay. *You're too dangerous for your own good, Batel.* 'In the morning,' she said, 'I'm going to speak to the local Arcana priest. They know the town. They may be able to provide help.'

Batel pursed his lips; on a normal day he would not object, but given the presence of Gulliver, not to mention the strange man in the bar, he doubted it was wise to ask questions of anyone. *Someone has let these smugglers enter and stay in this town.* 'Be careful, Marie.'

'You suspect something?'

'A cleric asking too many questions might create unnecessary aggravation.' He glanced towards the window and the world which lay beyond. *This town is being built on a corrupt foundation. Smugglers and Arcana's Shadow have a firm chokehold.*

'I can look after myself. I have magic too,' Marie reminded.

'I know.'

Marie smiled. 'What do we tell the others? They will have questions of us speaking tonight.'

'Tell them you needed to speak to me on urgent Church of Arcana business. They won't ask more after hearing that.' Batel knew how to play politics if needed.

Marie nodded. 'I agree. Now, if you don't mind, I'm tired, I need to sleep.'

Without another word, Batel stood and made his way to door. 'Good night,' he murmured as he opened the door, closing it gently behind him.

On the landing, he leant over the banister and scanned the bar below. Who knew what lay ahead? He steeled his heart. *If a Cockatrice was fearsome and took all our might to kill, what will it take to kill a Gryphon? We were lucky in Licorne.* He sighed heavily. *Well, tomorrow, we come face to face with the King of the Land and Sky.*

4 – Le Gryphon à L'Affût

The Next Morning – Woodland to the South-East of Sirene

In the cool morning air, Johan marched ahead through the muddied forest path, kicking stones and avoiding the piles of horse manure that littered the road. Sunlight filtered through the treetops and glistened on the dew drops which clung to spider's web and leaf alike. But beneath the tranquillity lurked a menace and Johan was prepared for it. In each hand, his enchanted blades were drawn ready for the fight. He did not entertain the idea of losing. *Henrik will hate it when he hears I slayed the beast. Killing a Cockatrice is one thing but killing a Gryphon will make him seethe with envy.*

Behind the giant, Carla, walking alongside Batel, was shouting directions. She knew the location of the Gryphon's lair. *We're getting close. I hope we're not foolishly throwing our lives away.*

She turned to Batel. 'I hope that strange halberd of yours works.'

'Would a bardiche be stranger?' Carla did not get chance to answer; Batel had come to a sudden stop. 'What's wrong?'

Johan was studying the ground in front of them. *Footprints. Fresh ones.* He bent down and stroked the mud. *These were made by man not beast. Who else is after the Gryphon?*

A deer ran in front of them and paused, unafraid.

Wild boar, indifferent to their presence, nosed in the undergrowth.

Carla noticed an abundance of woodland creatures in the vicinity. *They feel safe here. They do not feel threatened by us. Something has replaced us as king of the woods.*

'Everything alright, Johan?' Batel called.

'Are we the only ones Gulliver hired?'

'I don't know,' Batel answered before asking himself a new question. *Or does he have an abundance of men at his disposal?* The prestige of slaying a Gryphon would make legends of those who rid the town of its predator; they would be transformed from rogue smugglers to heroes. *We could be walking into an ambush.*

Carla equipped her bow and loaded it with an arrow from the quiver on her back. 'I'll provide cover.'

'Do you have enough magic to get us out of here?' Johan asked staring at the halberd.

Carla furrowed her brow. *What can that thing do?* She admired the magician's staff but the magician himself was an enigma – well-bred yet mixing with a giant and a thief yearning to be a scholar.

'Yes,' Batel reassured. 'I have magic enough. But once I signal the retreat, we get out. No questions asked.'

He stared at Carla.

He knew he had Johan's trust, his track record proved it, but he needed her assurances – she was as much an enigma to him as he was to her.

The archer presumed they would not continue forward without her word.

She smiled and even laughed. 'Very well, halberd boy.'

The Gryphon's Cave

The Gryphon stretched its giant eagle wings and flexed its talons. It bared its blade of a beak and lowered its bird-head to scratch its lion-body. The itch dispatched, it flexed its lion tale and strolled in front of the granite cave's mouth, the memory of being a lion prowling the open savannah retained in its flesh.

It sat now on its haunches at the mouth of its lair. Today was hunting day, or would have been if the Gryphon needed to exert effort to chase after prey. It found human flesh its preferred delicacy, a fact it savoured given they were ones who forced its existence into being. And those seeking glory were a considerate prey, walking up to its abode and presenting themselves ready for slaughter. Assailants had arrived that morning – some with swords in hand whilst others clamped daggers between their teeth – all eager to reclaim its guarded treasure. But the swords and the daggers driven into its flesh proved ineffective; its magical defences kicked in and ejected them. Wounds healed instantly and with a swipe of its vicious talons, the creature shredded its futile assailants to pieces. The Gryphon's beak was blood-stained from tearing flesh from the bone and peeling away tender meat. Even those who tried to run did not get far. The advantage of flight granted the Gryphon aerial dominance. It simply took to the air and dived down onto any fleeing smuggler before ending their life with a cruel precision. It was a most excellent harvest.

The Gryphon picked up what was left of the corpses and placed the shredded remains into the high branches of the trees around hm to pick away at when peckish. His store cupboard restocked, it found a fresh puddle of clean rainwater to wash the blood from its beak and feathers. It was in the process of licking its talons clean when something jabbed into its neck.

A piercing pain.

The Gryphon moaned. Its magical defences detected the foreign object and activated. The offending object was ejected and the creature extended its bird-neck to inspect an arrow that had fallen to the floor. It growled. More humans had come to test its patience. It turned to the bushes and bellowed – its snarl a fusion between an eagle's screech and a lion's roar.

'What are you doing?' Batel, eyes wide, mouthed at Carla.

Carla tried to justify herself. 'I should have pierced a vital vein.'

Johan was ready with his swords. *No need to hide anymore.* He leapt out of the bushes screaming his battle cry. 'Come and get me, you overgrown pigeon!'

The Gryphon made a baying noise that the humans interpreted as laughter then hunched its shoulders and extended its eagle-head forward. It found the giant curious. He was a different challenge to the ones it was used to.

From out of the cover of the trees, Batel and Carla stepped forward to stand with Johan.

The Gryphon angled his head towards Batel. The beast was not sizing him up for dinner but rather with intrigue. It took in the magician's scent and savoured it. Its behaviour unnerved Batel. *Can it smell magic? It's more intelligent than the Cockatrice.* The creature pawed the ground. It detected a peculiar stench coming from the enchanted halberds. They had killed a magically engineered beast before and the challenge excited it.

Johan stormed forth while Carla fired arrows into the air to provide him aerial cover. The arrows rained down upon the Gryphon, which did not dodge them. It allowed them to pierce its skin, causing mild irritation but insufficient to distract it – its magical defences repelled the arrows and healed the scratches that formed. Johan slashed his two blades, but the Gryphon beat its vast eagle-wings, gaining momentum and generating incredible lift which propelled it into the air high above the slashing blades.

It circled them.

Johan retreated to Batel's and Carla's position.

Arrows were fired into the beast's underbelly. They pierced it but not for long. All arrows were pushed out of the wounds and injuries were healed less than a minute later.

'What's it doing?' Johan screamed.

'It's toying with us,' Carla snarled.

Batel watched open-mouthed as the Gryphon gained more height. *Is it planning to crash down into us?*

The Gryphon roared and dived down head-first targeting Johan, who swung his sword but got his timing wrong. The creature's head slammed into his chest. His ribs rattled and shook; his internal organs ricocheted inside them. The beast's momentum threw the giant backward at a tremendous speed and floored him. Carla was caught in his path. She was knocked to the ground. Batel dashed over to help his fallen colleagues – *it's playing with its food* – and with a helping hand Carla and Johan slowly laboured to their feet. They were battered but could still fight. Above them, the Gryphon was gaining height again, ready to dive with another roar.

'Cover me! We're getting out of here!' Batel announced.

Johan and Carla took to the front again. 'Is that all you've got?' Johan screamed at the beast. 'I've played with kittens who hit harder than you!' The giant continued to be defiant.

Carla found herself too scared to move. *I'm going to die!*

Batel passed his fingertips over the halberd's axe-head. The blade glowed lilac as he prepared a grand swing. The Gryphon found this entertaining; it wanted to see what the magician would do.

Batel slashed the halberd. A ripple travelled forward through the air and stopped when it hit the trunk of a giant oak where the Gryphon stored its fresh meat. The bark of the tree became fluid to the eye, ebbing and flowing around a central point.

'Run!' Batel stumbled forward.

Carla caught him. 'What did you do?'

'I opened a portal out of here. Now go!'

Johan did not hesitate. He sprinted forward into the portal and vanished upon contact. Carla gawped, open-mouthed. *He's disappeared?*

The Gryphon's roar snapped her amazement. She sprinted towards the tree, closed her eyes and threw herself into the unknown. She was trusting Batel with her life. For a split second, she was aware of a cold sensation on her skin and then she disappeared.

Batel regained his composure. The Gryphon did not attack him. Instead, it proudly strutted around its domain. It nodded out of respect. Batel was confused. *Did it acknowledge my skill?*

The Gryphon, as if it knew what Batel was thinking, howled as Batel dashed through his portal. A loud rumble generated by a release in air pressure punctuated the portal's closure and echoed through the trees like thunder.

The Gryphon snarled. But there was no need to be greedy. It knew they would be back.

Outside The Humming Mermaid

The stone wall of the inn transformed into the same fluid consistency as the tree outside the Gryphon's lair. The portal spat out Johan, Carla and then Batel. Once again, it closed behind Batel and a rumble, this time reminiscent of horses hooves pounding the pavements, reverberated through the town.

Batel, Johan and Carla exhaled a huge sigh of relief. *At least we're not going to be a Gryphon's mid-morning snack.*

Carla put her hand against the stone wall. *It's back to normal. Not a sign of a portal left.* 'Handy trick, halberd boy.'

Johan, on the other hand, was more wary. 'That bird-cat was toying with us. What just happened?'

'Bird-cat ... that's what you've decided to call it? Really?' Carla was in no mood for jokes.

'Talitha will laugh,' Johan teased.

Batel ignored him and recomposed himself. Travelling through the portal gave him a headache. 'That Gryphon is smart and devious. We're not going to kill it easily. I need time to think.'

'What about Gulliver?' Carla reminded. 'He said we only have twenty-four hours to kill the beast. We stand no chance of killing that thing today!'

Batel did not answer, instead he stared blankly forward.

Johan recognised the signs; when Batel was thinking there no point asking him anything until he was done. *He's going to be like that all day.* 'I need a good beer. Want one?'

Carla suddenly became aware her mouth was dry. 'Definitely,' she said with a smile.

Together, they entered The Humming Mermaid, leaving Batel to think of a way out of their present predicament. *The Gryphon knows it is a prize to be hunted but it did not go for the kill when it had the chance – why? It seemed interested in my magic. It almost congratulated me for casting my spell.*

Batel leant back against the wall, temporarily defeated. *I hope Marie is having better luck than we are.*

5 – Les Agendas Secrets

The Church of Arcana – Sirene

This House of Arcana was smaller, dirtier and more run down than the one in Licorne, but Marie thought that was to be expected given its location; Sirene was not the decadent country village that lived off the patronage of a rich family – it was a port town falling into the laps of smugglers. *I do not envy the local priest's job. This is a challenging place to spread Arcana's message of peace and goodwill.*

The doors were unlocked. *They must be in.*

She entered the church to find the local priest practising his sermon for the next morning. A short, unassuming man with thinning grey hair, he bore the tired look of a man struggling to bear the burdens of responsibility. In a constant sweat, he seemed to be perpetually bent forward, although as soon as he spotted Marie his back straightened. At first, he realised he had forgotten to lock the doors and thought she was someone needing assistance with a minor quibble. Then, he took time to see who had entered. *A cleric? What is she doing here?*

'I was not expecting an inspection,' the priest stuttered nervously, folding his hands each over the other. 'This place is quite a mess. That extra funding I was promised has not yet arrived.'

'I'm only passing through.' Marie sought to calm the nervous priest. *He's a highly wired individual.* 'I sought a fellow believer's wisdom.'

'Oh? I see. Forgive my rudeness. I've got a lot on at the moment ... I'm Maubert, by the way.' The priest regained a modicum of composure and took a seat in the nearest pew. He was sweating profusely now and repeatedly wiped his brow.

Marie found his behaviour odd but did not question it. Instead, she quietly took a seat on an adjacent pew at an appropriate social distance and rested the staff beside her. 'I detected some strange magic in Sirene – perception-altering, quite rare, quite worrisome.'

Maubert leant forward and folded his hands over each other again. 'Perception-altering magic? How strange. Probably nothing to worry about. We have numerous types pass through here. I'm sure he's long gone.'

'He?' Marie did not recall mentioning anything about gender.

Maubert laughed an anxious laugh then coughed. 'Usually it's a man. I know, as a priest, I should not profile those who stray from Arcana's path, but it is unfortunately men that fall into criminality first.'

Marie trusted the words as the truth. *He's seen the worst of society. I can see the hope draining from his eyes.*

Maubert started to relax. *It's fine. She suspects nothing.*

A gold chain slipped down his arm and came to rest on his wrist. Marie pursed her lips; a priest, when on duty, should minimise personal affectations let alone one so flashy and gaudy. 'Is that a personal item?'

Maubert's anxiety took hold. *What do I do? She'll report me! They'll investigate me and I'll get excommunicated!* His cheeks reddened. *Think! Think! What do I say?* 'It was my mother's.'

'I see,' said Marie, who decided to take Maubert at face value. *We all attach value to personal objects. I am not one to judge.* 'But maybe best to keep it hidden.'

'Yes!' Maubert could not hide his nerves much longer; they were waiting to erupt into a full confession. *She knows! She knows! What do I do? Keep calm. She came in to talk about magic.* He made an effort to temper his voice. 'To return to the matter in hand, I've not noticed anyone using perception-altering magic but I'll ask some questions. There might be an innocent explanation.'

Marie stood up and bowed graciously in thanks. She grabbed her staff and smiled. *Strange man but he's clearly overly stressed and over-worked.* She departed leaving Maubert to his duties completely oblivious to the priest's true thoughts.

Maubert leant back in the pew and started at the vaulted ceiling. *Blessed are the innocent in their naivety. I might fool her but I won't fool anyone with any street sense. I must tell La Roue. He'll know what to do.*

The Docks – Sirene

Talitha stalked Gulliver with a keen eye. She watched as he waltzed through a group of sailors with a pronounced swagger, unaware he was being followed, but then Talitha always kept out of view; there was no need for her invisibility potion yet, but she was getting bored of hiding behind a series of empty barrels. The air was brisk. She was losing the feeling in her fingers. She peered out from behind a whiskey cask. *Why is he shouting at sailors? They're not even his crew, just random people wondering what they did wrong. They look so confused.* She sighed. Following a smuggler captain was proving less exciting than she imagined it would be. *Where's the thrill? The sense of danger?* Then again, now she thought about it, Talitha realised she was missing the point. Gulliver was shouting at these men because he didn't have a crew of his own. *Is he a one man show? Don't captains need an actual crew?*

'Spying on Renard as well?' a male voice behind her asked. Talitha started, her trance-like focus on Gulliver broken. She went to draw her enchanted dagger out of its sheath on her belt, but the owner of the voice grabbed her hand and forced the dagger back inside. No matter how much Talitha tried, she could not overpower him.

When she dared to look up, she saw someone the same age as her; he was only a boy, really. But he was handsome – soft cheeks, round face and a sense of adventure lurking within his eyes. A funny feeling buzzed inside Talitha. *He's cute. Deceptively so.*

He let go of her hand.

Talitha did not pull the dagger out. 'Who are you?'

'Isaac,' said the young man. *Why is she looking at me that way? Is she OK? Why have her cheeks gone red?*

Talitha pulled herself together enough to process what Isaac had said. 'Wait, who's Renard?'

Isaac pointed at Gulliver through the gaps between the barrels. 'Him!'

'No! That's Gulliver!' Talitha insisted.

'I think I would recognise my own father.'

Father? He's Gulliver's son. Wait! Is he saying that's not Gulliver over there? Talitha's head started to hurt. 'Who's Renard then?'

Isaac's frustration slipped through. He bit his lip. 'My father's first mate. He's wearing his jacket and pretending to be him. Pretending to be captain.'

So Batel's not being dealing with Gulliver, instead, his first-mate Renard has been acting as an imposter. Talitha realised Batel, and by extension herself, Marie and Johan, had been deceived.

'Why are you interested in Renard?' Isaac asked.

'He hired us. We hunt monsters, you see,' Talitha boasted.

Monsters? She means the Gryphon. So, Renard is after father's treasure. Isaac saw his chance to get assistance. He found himself unexpectedly alone in Sirene – no allies and no family. 'We?'

'I'm the-' Talitha paused. *I can't tell him I'm a thief. It would be massive turn off.* 'Um ... uh ... I'm the scout!' *Smooth, Talitha. Smooth.*

'And who else is in your group?'

'There's a giant with a drinking problem who wields two swords. A cleric who's incredibly uptight. Then, we've got a halberd-wielding magician who takes himself too seriously.'

As she spoke, Talitha kept playfully tapping Isaac's arms. He tried his best to ignore her. *Don't engage with her. Not until this mess with Renard is resolved. I can't be distracted.* 'Can I meet your ... uh ... associates?'

Talitha bounced on the spot. 'Sure. We're staying at The Humming Mermaid.'

'Great. I'll come after dusk.' Isaac smiled. It was pained and awkward. He was trying too hard. *Keep cool. She's just a woman.*

Talitha found him sweet. *He smiled? That's a good sign, right?*

Isaac didn't know what else to say and departed as quickly as he arrived.

Talitha grinned, then gave one final glance towards Renard through the barrels. *We're close to figuring you out. And when I tell Batel, he'll have you wrapped around his little finger.*

6 – L'Influence du Vendeur

An Alley near the Church of Arcana – Sirene

La Roue's magic granted him extraordinary confidence. His perception-altering spell set him apart from his competitors and allowed him to dominate his niche in the market. Only occasionally did people perceive his presence and then they would dismiss it as nothing more than a trick of the light. La Roue allowed himself a smile. He appreciated his anonymity; enjoyed the ability to roam with freedom. It was no coincidence that his nickname was 'the wheel'.

Inspecting his carefully taken notes, La Roue tapped his pen on the paper. *The smugglers are getting restless. They're too jumpy. They're making mistakes. New management is always eager to make bold decisions, even when their coffers are rapidly draining, and that makes them my ideal prey.*

It was at that moment that Maubert arrived at their designated rendezvous, almost tripping over himself in his hurry.

La Roue lowered the perception veil around him and studied the sweating man now standing in front of him. *Why are corrupt Arcana priests always so needy?*

'We have a problem. There's a cleric, a clever one,' Maubert blurted. 'She came and asked questions ... About you. And your magic.'

La Roue snapped his ledger shut. *So, she did notice me last night. Clearly she has more nous than this dribbling buffoon.* 'I presume you answered her questions calmly and sensibly?'

The priest pulled at his collar.

La Roue did not need his question answering. *It was cruel of the Church of Arcana to assign a weakling to a potential smuggler's paradise. It was disappointing how easily it was for me to wrap you around my little finger.* He pinched the skin on the bridge of his nose. 'You do not fill me with confidence, Maubert.'

'What do I do?' Maubert pleaded.

La Roue sprang to his feet and grabbed the priest by the scruff of his neck. 'Listen here, I'm a businessman. I analyse markets. I identify demand. I meet supply. For that, I need a marketplace. Sirene is perfect – a free port that has access to the La Mer Étroite. I sell monsters. I do so with discretion.'

He dropped Maubert who fell to the sawdust-covered floor. 'Dispose of the cleric as you have disposed of the others who have asked you awkward questions before.'

Maubert gulped. 'But ... but ... a cleric of Arcana?'

La Roue laughed. 'I am a devotee of the free market. I hold no faith in your goddess, neither do I pretend to be virtuous. I'm not the hypocrite here.'

'I'll ... I'll poison her then,' Maubert snivelled like the meek coward La Roue knew him to be.

La Roue placed a hand on his shoulder. 'Good. And remember, be careful. I can disappear without people realising I was even here. You, on the other hand, are a trusted public figure. If you're exposed, you cannot hide. And when you're being lynched and swinging from a tree, I'll be standing in the crowd laughing.'

The colour drained from Maubert's face.

La Roue shook his head at him and left him on the verge of vomiting. 'Meet me at the dock at daybreak.' *Now I swindle the smuggler.*

The Docks – Sirene

La Roue could tell Renard was entering this crucial phase of the transaction from a position of weakness. His communications had become more desperate; Renard was a man clinging to power and it was falling through his fingers faster than sand from a leaky hourglass. As he strode across the deserted dock towards La Roue, he was escorted by Henrik – his hired personal protection, who came to stand in front of La Roue, his massive arms folded across his chest. La Roue smirked. *Your hired muscle does not scare me.* La Roue erected his salesman's persona and began his routine of nauseous faux pleasantries. 'Your order arrives at dawn. I thank you for opting for our premium service.'

Renard emerged from behind his hired help. 'It better arrive when you say! That Gryphon has been disturbing my plans for too long now. I've sent the last twelve of my men this morning to retrieve the treasure. None have returned, have they Henrik?'

'It would appear not.'

La Roue suppressed a laugh. *He sent his own men? He might as well feed the Gryphon personally. And now his men are dead. Well, I take no responsibility.* 'The Gryphon is a top of the range creature. I'm sure the alchemists back in the laboratories are pleased by the beast's performance.'

Renard growled. 'Bloody pain it is.'

'Well, it is designed to guard treasure,' La Roue reminded. He noticed Henrik remained silent. *He's probably paid per syllable.*

'As long as my order, when it arrives, kills the beast,' Renard observed.

'Indeed.' La Roue fake-smiled.

'You might be interested to know that I hired a magician to kill the Gryphon. Hopefully, the creature tore his throat out.' He paused; smirked. 'The magician in question killed one of your beasts, didn't he?'

He hired Batel? La Roue grimaced. *That's not good. Batel is getting too close for comfort.* 'We all encounter opposition and bad luck from time to time, but I assure you, we are confident in the quality of our products.'

Renard rolled his eyes. 'I'm sure you are.'

'If that concludes our business today, I will see you at dawn at the dock for the delivery of your order.' La Roue bowed his head and left. *I need to choose my next move carefully. If Batel gets hold of Maubert, he'll spill everything. I need Renard and Maubert to hold out until tomorrow morning. Once the beast has been delivered, I can start the clean-up.*

Alone with Henrik, Renard felt the pressure of the gamble he had taken. *I've spent all my gold. All my men are dead. Maybe Gulliver was right, maybe I was never going to be a good captain. No! I can rise above this. I've bought a monster. Not gifted one. I'll claim the treasure for my own. Great men take risks.*

Henrik cleared his throat.

'A reminder, Captain. If I do not get paid by midday tomorrow, I'm leaving.'

'Do not worry, Henrik. Tomorrow, we'll never have to worry about gold again.'

7 – Le Patron Mécontent

Batel's Room, The Humming Mermaid – Sirene

Batel had locked himself away in his room. When he returned from his encounter with The Gryphon, he crashed on his bed and had since been staring, blank-eyed, at the ceiling. Generating a magical portal was exhausting. *I need one of Marie's energy elixirs but if I ask for one she'll be angry with me. She's already worried about me. She doesn't want me to get myself killed, but the truth is we need days, no, weeks of preparation to stand a chance against that creature.*

He rubbed his eyes. *I had a twenty-four-hour deadline to kill it. It was an impossible deadline. I was set up to fail.*

He blinked furiously. *What am I going to do?*

An idea flew into his head.

Leaping out of bed, he pulled out a bag from underneath, opened the lock and began rifling through for something he had not seen for a while. *There it is.*

He grabbed a folded piece of paper – the purchase slip from the Telliers for their Cockatrice – unfolded it and scanned to the bottom of the page. *Who signed the document for Arcana's Shadow?* He flicked the paper with his finger. *There it is. La Roue's signature.*

He eased himself down on to the edge of his bed. *La Roue is in Sirene. There are seeds of doubt I sow. That's my bargaining chip.*

Main Bar, The Humming Mermaid

'Another!' Johan had lost count of how many pints he had drunk.

Carla dared not to count. *He's really going at it.* 'You are going to stop, right?'

'You drink when you win. You drink when you lose.' Johan shared his philosophy for life.

'That's addiction,' Talitha sniped from the corner, her eyes never leaving the page of her makeshift bestiary to which she was adding details of their encounter with the Gryphon.

Carla marvelled at the way her quill generated its own ink. *These are strange people ... and carrying on as if nothing has happened. I'm too shaky to even hold a pen.* She glanced over at Johan. 'How are you not traumatised?'

Johan paused. He wanted to summon his best words. He cleared his throat.

Carla leant in, eager to hear.

Johan prepared himself for his message. 'You're alive.'

Carla sighed heavily. 'But we could have been killed.'

'Don't discount the fact we're still alive. I was nearly killed once by a chicken-dragon.'

Chicken-dragon? Carla grimaced. 'What are you talking about?'

'The Cockatrice.' Talitha stopped writing and turned back to the first entry in her notebook, then slid it across the table to the archer.

Carla read intently. *A chicken fused with a dragon. Highly vicious. Murderous. Slashes with its claws. Powerful. Beak tears flesh.* Carla did not know whether to laugh or cry. She read on. *These monsters are designed to be ruthless predators. They could devastate wildlife and livestock if left unchecked.*

Carla pushed the bestiary back to its author. 'How does the Gryphon compare?'

Johan leant back in his chair, stretched his arms high above his head, then sighed heavily. 'Smarter. Crueller. Stronger. It's a dangerous bird-cat.' He burped. The all-day drinking was catching up with him.

'You can't call it that,' Carla complained.

'Too late!' Talitha announced. 'It's in the bestiary. It's official now!'

'But it's such a stupid name.' Her voice was rising. 'Can't it be changed?'

'No!' Talitha closed her notebook and held it tightly against her chest.

Carla opened her mouth to complain, but Johan leant forward, resting his large arms on the table, and looked her in the eye. She shrank in her place. *What's he going to say?*

'You must relax. If you don't, the Gryphon has already won the second round.'

Carla growled. *He's probably right.* 'I need a good night's sleep.'

But Talitha was off in her own world. *What else could I call a Gryphon? An eagle-lion? An Eagon? No. A Ligle? I like Ligle.* 'Can I call it a "Ligle"?'

'No!' Carla snapped but she could not hold a stern expression. A smile cracked through. She shook her head. *It's not worth it. Not my bestiary. She can write what she wants.*

Batel came down the stairs, his enchanted halberd his steadfast companion. Before leaving for his meeting, he checked in. 'Are we alright?'

'Fine,' Johan merrily hummed.

'Doing better,' Carla confessed. 'What have you been doing?'

'Thinking. Planning.'

'He's been asleep.' Johan joked.

Batel rolled his eyes. He did not dignify the joke with a response. 'Has anyone seen Marie?'

'She's in her room, praying,' Carla relayed.

'Then I'll talk to her when I get back. I'm off to get shouted at by Gulliver.'

Talitha perked up. She slammed her bestiary shut. 'Before you go, there's something you need to know. I met Gulliver's son.'

Batel was intrigued. 'And?'

'Well, apart from being deceptively cute, he told me his father is missing. The first-mate Renard is impersonating Gulliver. You've been dealing with an imposter.'

All of them ignored the 'cute' comment. They were too busy taking onboard the new information.

Batel smiled. *You've made my day, Talitha. I've been dealing with a fake captain. That sly fox.* 'Very good work, Talitha. Reliable as always.'

Talitha beamed.

Carla shook her head in disbelief. *She does not strike me as reliable.*

'His name is Isaac,' Talitha went on. 'He wants to speak to us tonight.'

Batel was cheered. *I've been given ammunition.* He knew his forthcoming meeting would start poorly. After all, failure to kill the Gryphon meant he had failed to meet his end of the bargain. But now he was armed with crucial information. *The fox is caught out in the open, alone.*

The Docks – Sirene

Renard and Henrik saw Batel approaching. They were eager to make this quick. 'Did you kill the Gryphon?'

'No, Renard.' Batel saw the smuggler's face drop at the mention of his real name.

Henrik drew breath. *His day had just got worse.*

Renard flared his nostrils. 'How? How do you know, magician?'

'People talk. People listen.' Batel dodged the question with an antagonising smile.

'You think you're funny?' Renard went to hit Batel only to be held back by Henrik. He glared at the giant and seethed but could not break his restraint. Then, reason caught up with his rage. *I did pay Henrik to protect me. Even from myself.* He took a deep breath and calmed himself down. Warily, Henrik let him go.

Renard straightened his black leather jacket and addressed Batel from a safe distance. 'Well, since you failed to kill the Gryphon, I won't pay you. Now, get lost!'

Batel had no intention of leaving. 'I would leave Sirene if I were you. Before La Roue cons you out of the rest of your gold.'

Henrik winced. Batel figured he was already too late. *What have you done, Renard?*

'You know La Roue?' Renard found himself surprised.

'I'm trying to bring him down. His organisation is too dangerous to be allowed to continue trading. But I need help to do this.' Batel offered out the hand of friendship, a new partnership.

Renard stared at the inviting hand and laughed derisively. 'You cannot be serious?' He gathered saliva and spat at Batel, who lurched out of the way. Renard sneered. 'No deal, magician. You're on your own.'

Batel withdrew his hand. 'I'm not surprised. Disappointed but not surprised.' He clocked Henrik's disapproving shake of the head behind Renard's back. *At least he understands.*

Renard turned to leave. 'Tomorrow, at dawn, all my problems will be solved. La Roue has earnt my trust.'

Renard's parting shot rang in Batel's ears. He departed chuntering under his breath. *I should have never hired that arrogant magician.* Henrik followed swiftly behind, shaking his head in anticipation of what was to come.

Tomorrow? Batel remembered Renard imposing a strict deadline on their initial deal. *He's ordered something from La Roue, hasn't he?* He walked with great speed and purpose back to The Humming Mermaid. *Tomorrow could be carnage.*

8 – Le Prêtre Corrompu

Marie's Room – The Humming Mermaid

'Come in!' Marie had finished her daily prayers and welcomed her visitor, knowing who it was from the way in which the Sangterre inside the orb of her staff swirled.

Batel walked in, pleased to see a friendly face. 'I've recovered from the exertions of this morning.'

'I'm pleased ... and you're safe and sound, that Gryphon sounds awfully frightening. How did your meeting go?'

'Not great. I think they've bought their own monster to kill the Gryphon,' Batel relayed.

Marie furrowed her brow. 'What do we do?'

'We have until dawn to think of a plan. Talitha found a useful source of information. He's coming to talk with us tonight and he could be the wildcard we require.'

'That good. I'll try to make it back for then.' Marie was conscious of time.

Batel arched an eyebrow. 'Where are you going?'

'Maubert asked me to go to the church and assist him in the writing of a sermon,' she enthused. Travelling meant she had no religious community of her own and, whilst she put great credence on her work, she had imagined herself contributing to a dedicated group of Arcana worshippers rather than chasing around the country putting a stop to monsters.

This late in the day? It's nearly nightfall. Maubert's request did not sit well with Batel. 'What was Maubert like earlier today?'

'Strange fellow. He seemed nervous, anxious. I think Sirene is a tough assignment.' Marie laughed. 'He was wearing a gold chain around his wrist. He was embarrassed to be seen with it.'

Batel did not find Maubert's description neither charming nor amusing. *He sounds defensive. He's hiding something.* 'Why did he have a gold chain?'

'A family gift.' Marie's trust was implicit.

She has no reason to doubt Maubert. He's a priest of Arcana. But I don't trust him. Batel twisted his lips to one side, unsure what to say. He knew Marie would defend a fellow Arcana devotee without hard evidence to challenge that position but he worried for her. 'Can't I convince you to wait until morning? That way we will know what we're dealing with.'

'I'll be fine. We said we have until dawn tomorrow and I know how to look after myself.' Marie was not going to ignore her calling.

Batel did not argue. He never doubted Marie's power. She was a more than capable spellcaster as well as a cleric of Arcana. It was less honourable, more cowardly forms of attack he was worried about. But he kept his counsel and watched as Marie departed with a spring in her step. *I know Marie sees herself as a priestess of Arcana someday. She's travelling to learn, to gain experience and I can't deny her that, but La Roue has his claws all over Sirene. You can't import monsters without people noticing. If I were him, I would bribe top public officials to buy their silence. And Maubert is ideally placed to turn a blind eye. I wouldn't be surprised if that gold chain was a gift he should not have accepted.*

Batel had a choice to make. *The worst thing I could do is nothing. If I'm wrong about Maubert, the worst thing I need to do is apologise to him and deal with a severely miffed Marie. Sorry, Marie, I know this is important to you but I must check Maubert out for myself.*

The Church of Arcana – Sirene

'Ah! There you are!' Maubert declared as he caught sight of Marie approaching the doors he had left open for her arrival. He hurried towards her as she made her way towards the church and, with open arms, ushered her in. 'Come, come, you are most welcome.' Marie nodded and passed through the holy portal. 'I have poured the wine,' he gushed, leading her down the aisle to where he had placed two goblets of red sacramental wine on a small table covered in a white, lace cloth. *Forgive me, Arcana, but I must do this to protect what I have built here. May she find peace inside your beating heart within the planet as one of your treasured children. I know I never will.*

He picked up the two goblets and handed one to her. Marie gladly accepted it, although she thought the offering strange. *Come on! Drink!* Maubert watched as Marie raised the cup to her lips. *I'm sorry, cleric.*

'Arcana is a complex goddess,' Batel's voice boomed from the far end of the nave.

Marie lowered her goblet. *Batel?*

Maubert span around to see who had the nerve to interrupt him.

'Arcana is fondly known as the Goddess of Life, the giver of harvests, bestower of fertilities,' Batel continued as he made his way down the aisle towards them. 'But if you read the holy texts carefully, it states that Arcana is also a Goddess of Death.' Batel drew to a halt directly in front of Maubert's face and glared right into his quivering eyes.

Marie baulked. 'Batel? What's wrong?'

Sweat beaded on Maubert's face. *Arcana has judged me. I'm found guilty.* He laughed nervously; his voice cracked. 'You're well-read, magician, but what has this got to do with anything? I merely asked for assistance with my upcoming sermon.'

'Batel! You better have a good reason!' Marie scowled. *He's being overly paranoid.*

'Drink from her goblet.' Batel called the priest's bluff. He slammed the end of the halberd into the floor. 'Now!'

In his panic, Maubert dropped his goblet, red sacramental wine spilling everywhere, then barged past Batel and ran out of the church. He abandoned his calling, his duty.

Marie put down her goblet quickly. She felt light-headed. She had to sit down. *I ... I almost died?* She went pale – no longer comfortable in her white, cleric's robes. 'It was poisoned?'

Batel took no pleasure neither did he gloat. He had hoped he was wrong and was simply being paranoid but he needed to be sure. 'From what you said, it sounded as if Maubert behaved suspiciously and I ... well, I am responsible for your safety. I had to call his bluff.' He paused. 'Don't worry. I was prepared to grovel if I was wrong.'

Marie bowed her head. 'Thank you. You are my protector.'

She fought the urge to rush forward and kiss Batel on the lips. *A cleric must be above such urges. Clear the thought from your mind!* She tightened her grip on her staff. *Compose yourself, woman. Batel doesn't even notice you.*

But Batel was already on his way out of the church. 'Come on. We have work to do.' *We're making progress. We're removing the corruption from Sirene one piece at a time.*

9 – L'Historie du Fils

Main Bar, The Humming Mermaid – Sirene

Isaac's footsteps were cautious.

He was taking a risk showing himself in a public place.

He had been careful not to alert Renard of his presence in Sirene but he had to act. *I'll find out what happened to you, Father.*

'Isaac!' Talitha waved from across the bar.

Isaac inhaled deeply. *So much for a stealthy approach.*

He walked towards Talitha and then noticed Johan standing beside her.

Just one glance and he backstepped. *He's big. His forearms are bigger than my head.*

'Come on! We'll talk upstairs. Everyone is waiting for you.' Talitha led the way.

Out of politeness, Johan waited until Isaac started to follow her. He could see from the way their visitor had been staring at him – eyes wide, mouth slack – that he was intimidated.

Johan smirked.

He enjoyed playing the role of bodyguard.

Issac was funnelled into Batel's room. He found himself standing in the middle of the floor plan, surrounded by an eclectic, not to mention unusual group of people. *There's a hunter, a cleric and a magician, as well as a giant? Talitha looks like the most normal one here but even she's eccentric.* As if she knew he was thinking about her, Talitha gave him a reassuring nod before she took her seat. The others, who arranged themselves around the room, regarded him with mistrust, bordering on disdain. It was clear they were not going to take any nonsense; their patience was wearing thin.

Batel cleared his throat. 'You're the son of Gulliver, the real Gulliver?'

Isaac suspected he was being interrogated. *I've done nothing wrong here.* 'Yes, I am his son.'

'Then tell me,' Carla asked, speaking on behalf of the people of Sirene, 'What is Renard planning to do at dawn?'

'I don't know.'

'That's not good enough!' Marie slammed her staff on to the floorboards. Isaac recoiled. Even Talitha, Johan and Carla were surprised. This was not the calm and placid Marie they were used to.

Batel waved his hand, signalling her to keep calm.

She took a deep breath and bowed her head. 'My apologies. The local priest just tried to poison me, so I'm understandably on edge.'

Glances were exchanged around the room. This was news to everyone except Batel, who sensed the need to make things less confrontational. 'How about you tell us everything you know, Isaac? Start from the beginning.'

Isaac looked up at the eyes staring at him and shuffled in place. He gave a concerned glance towards Talitha. He did not trust them.

'They're good people, Isaac.'

He swallowed his doubts and concerns. 'My father, the real Gulliver, made a deal with a cruel Mercian Lord, who mercilessly overtaxed the poor and kept some of the gold hidden from the royal coffers. He bought a Gryphon from Arcana's Shadow to guard his hoard.'

The room fell unnaturally silent.

Isaac knew not to expect sympathy when describing his father. *He's a smuggler. People don't like smugglers.* Yet the group did its best to hide their initial feelings. They understood Isaac was only a boy. Talitha kicked at a chair leg; by comparison her achievements in thievery felt small. *I have a lot to learn.* Marie, who guessed what Talitha was thinking, had to make an effort to suppress another outburst. *Why am I throwing myself into the criminal underworld? What happened to the righteous path?*

Johan coughed to break the silence.

Batel nodded. 'Carry on.'

'The Mercian Lord faced a peasants' revolt. Fearing for his treasure, he hired my father to smuggle it out of the country. La Roue suggested it was brought to Sirene. So, we did what we were paid to do. We moved the treasure and hid it in the forest. The Gryphon answered to my father. He became the beast's master.'

Master? Batel found himself truly perplexed. *The Gryphon has a master? It answered to Gulliver?* He had to stay focused on the here and now. 'What happened?'

'The peasants' revolt succeeded and the Mercian Lord was hanged, beheaded and dismembered, then burnt to ash.'

All sat less comfortably in their seats. Carla growled under her breath. *Sirene has nothing to do with Mercian squabbles. Why bring their problems here?* Marie grew even more irritable. *Both Etellia and Mercia have suffered from the heresy of Arcana's Shadow.* Batel accepted the cold reality. *La Roue won't care as long as he's getting paid.*

'My father was due to meet me in Sirene to reclaim the treasure and free the Gryphon but he never arrived. Instead, Renard showed up pretending to be him, he was even wearing his favourite jacket. I ... I-' Isaac could not finish, the thought too horrible.

'You think Renard mutinied and killed your father?' Carla finished Isaac's sentence for him.

Isaac nodded once.

Talitha held his hand reassuringly. 'It's OK.'

Marie could not believe her eyes. *She's doing my job.*

'Renard was always jealous and petty,' Isaac went on. 'He wanted to be captain, but my father laughed at that idea. Something dramatic must have happened for him to take over command of the ship.'

Gulliver had not been wrong. Batel had his own judgement validated.

'We'll stop Renard,' Talitha promised.

'Thank you.' Isaac found Talitha sincere.

Johan, who had been staying silent until now, leant forward in his seat and raised a finger to announce he was about to speak. 'How much gold are we talking about here?'

Isaac took a deep breath. 'Enough to finance a new township.'

A collective gasp echoed around the room.

Batel stepped forward. 'We need to stop Renard acquiring that treasure. I suspect he's bought his own monster from La Roue to kill the Gryphon.'

Own monster? Isaac had grown fond of the Gryphon during his brief time with it. 'The Gryphon's not a monster. It's a living, breathing creature.'

'It's killed good hunters. Good friends of mine.' Carla fired a shot across Isaac's bow.

Batel threw her a stare. He did not need to say anything. She recognised his command to stay quiet and listen. Such interventions would not be helpful.

'The Gryphon is an manmade abomination. It is a weapon, a tool,' Batel explained.

But that did not condemn the beast in Isaac's eyes. 'It has the right to life as we do. Technically, it is my responsibility now. It knows me. It trusts me. It will help us to stop Renard.'

Carla refused to stay quiet; this was too important. 'Can you be sure?'

'It's our best chance fighting what Renard has planned.'

Logical thinking started to kick into the room. Talitha's face softened. And then Johan nodded. Even Marie agreed. *If the Gryphon can help us stop Renard, La Roue and Maubert, then it will be doing good.*

But Batel refused to join in with the consensus. 'Sirene is a victim of a larger, nationwide problem. The Gryphon is a symptom. There needs to be a cure.'

'But can you even kill it?' Isaac retorted.

Batel smiled. Then laughed. As much as he was an idealist, he was a pragmatist. *He's got me there. We do not have the right equipment to take on a Gryphon.* He picked up his halberd which was resting against the wall. 'We're trusting you, Isaac. You approach the Gryphon at your own risk, do you understand?'

'I understand.' Isaac affirmed his faith in the Gryphon.

'So what's the plan, halberd boy?' Carla asked.

Marie hid an indignant snarl. *I hate that nickname. Stop flirting with him.*

Batel assessed his available options. *We've got six people. Some are fighters. Others are not. If Renard has purchased his own monster, we must be careful.* 'Marie, Carla, Isaac and myself will go to the Gryphon's grotto at dawn.'

The three of them all agreed.

'Isaac, we'll cover you.' Isaac smiled; reassured. Batel turned to address Carla's concerns. 'Carla, have your arrows ready.' She nodded. The magician turned to Marie. 'Be ready to cast a well-chosen spell.' Batel saw the cleric smile; encouraged. Then, he turned to Talitha. 'See if you can find La Roue. He should have some sort of ledger. Steal it. If we believe Renard, La Roue should be at the docks at dawn.' Batel trusted his operative who played in the shadows.

Talitha accepted the task with glee and anticipation. *The thief gets to play.* But Isaac felt nervous, his hands constantly fidgeting. He was still a child but he needed to be brave.

Carla reconciled the conflicting emotions in her heart. *The Gryphon is a monster. It has killed good hunters. But it is a victim of circumstance. Renard and La Roue are the true poisoners of Sirene. They corrupted Maubert.*

Marie steeled herself. The Gryphon was a different animal to a Cockatrice. *Remember, this is my calling. To travel from town to town to ensure Arcana's message is heard. Sirene needs saving. Maubert is a symptom of what ails it. We must remove the chokehold Arcana's Shadow has over the land.*

This left Johan, who silently sat on the edge of the bed awaiting the correct orders. His eyes had not broken contact from Batel. *I want you to say it, Batel. I need you to say it.*

'Whilst we head to the Gryphon's lair, you distract Renard and Henrik. It's time you two squared off against each other,' Batel said with a smile.

The giant stood up. 'Thank you.'

'Be careful, Johan.' Batel warned.

'I will.' Johan respected his dear friend's concern.

'Talitha!' Marie called out surprising her.

What have I done now? Talitha was too tired to be lectured. Instead, when she looked up at Marie she was greeted by a smile. *That's creepy. I don't like it.*

'Do you have an invisibility potion?' Marie asked.

'Yes. And my enchanted dagger.' Talitha saw Isaac's astonishment as she put the dagger in its sheath on her belt.

She's got an invisibility potion? She's full of surprises. Isaac found himself gawking.

'You need more. La Roue uses perception-altering magic to hide in plain sight.' Marie placed the orb in her staff within touching distance of Talitha's nose. The Sangterre inside swirled. A shining light caressed Talitha's face and then faded.

Talitha madly inspected herself. *Have I been blessed with magic? Have I been transformed? Can I cast spells now?* As her hands checked different parts of her body, the crushing reality set in. 'You've not enabled me to use magic, have you?'

'I cannot give talent to those who do not possess it.' Marie allowed herself a moment of superiority.

Carla could not help but admire Marie's feisty nature. *She's trained hard to suppress it but she's not a saint.* Batel and Johan smiled. *She's been waiting ages to use that punchline.*

Isaac wanted to defend Talitha but knew it was not his place. *I don't understand their banter.*

Talitha needed no further invitation to retaliate. 'I always knew you were all flashing lights and no substance.'

'Ah! I must disagree,' Marie decreed. 'I've allowed you to see. You should be able to see La Roue, no problem.'

'You mean I can see through his perception-changing thing?' Talitha gave credit where credit was due.

Marie sighed. 'Yes.' *She's still a long way to go if she is to understand magic.*

'We've only got one shot at this. We all know what we must do,' Batel rallied. He looked at everyone in this room and gave them a respectful bow of his head. *I'm creating an organisation of my own. It grows stronger with each adventure. We will knock La Roue off his perch.*

10 – La Livraison du Monstre

Dawn the Next Day, the Docks – Sirene

'You're a feisty one.'

La Roue was in awe of the hidden beast chained inside the large crate thrashing against its prison walls, trying to break free. *Stupid beast is confused and starved of light and food.* He laughed. *You can't wait to be unleashed on an unsuspecting village, can you?* He turned his attention to the dock and inhaled the sea breeze. *Today is going to be a good day.* He shouted up to the gunnel of the barnacle-encrusted ship moored to his side. 'Has the payment from Renard been loaded?'

A sailor overseeing the shipment answered his boss's call. 'Yes, Sir! We're ready to go.'

'Good.' La Roue smirked.

'Sir! Will we be sailing straight away?'

La Roue turned to the crate behind him. 'No, I've got something to do.'

'Are ... Are you sure, Sir? If today goes wrong, there might two monsters rampaging in Sirene.'

La Roue glared at the upstart sailor. *I wish I could throw you overboard. Or feed you to the beast.* Instead, he laughed smugly and turned up his nose. 'No-one will see me.'

Several metres away, hiding behind a stack of barrels, Talitha stared in horror at the crate as it rocked. *What's inside? Did Renard order a monster?* A bellow came from inside which confirmed her suspicions and she cowered lower behind the barrels, and just in time because as she did she spotted a man approaching.

La Roue saw him too. *And the pretender has arrived.*

Renard arrived at the appointed time; Henrik joining him. Both marvelled at the imprisoned beast's rage, although Henrik found Renard's fascination with it bordered on the disturbing. He stepped back as Renard stepped forward. *I feel my investment was wise. I trust this beast's rage.*

La Roue approached and Renard offered his congratulatory hand, which La Roue accepted with a crushing grip. 'Why call yourself "La Roue"? It's not a name any mother would give.'

La Roue let go of the smuggler's hand. 'The wheel of business always turns. It transcends countries. And I keep it turning.'

Renard shrugged off the sales pitch. 'Is the beast ready?'

La Roue clapped his hands together. 'Yes!'

Sailors from the ship which belonged to Arcana's Shadow were on hand to open the crate. They were nervous. They took things slowly. They did not want to unwittingly become breakfast. Yet, when the wooden panel was opened, the beast inside was surprisingly reluctant to make its entrance. It backed itself into a corner and pawed the ground. One of the crew decided to reboard the ship and fetch a chunk of meat, which he threw down onto the ground in front of the crate and then ran away as fast as his sea legs would allow.

In dawn's light, first in shadow, barely visible, the beast reluctantly revealed itself.

A Cockatrice had been bought to Sirene.

Talitha covered her mouth to quieten her gasp. *No! He didn't! He can't be that stupid!*

The half-chicken, half-dragon bellowed its strange, hybrid roar that was some bizarre combination of a deep hissing and the rooster's morning call.

'Magnificent!' Renard announced.

Henrik backstepped ready to run, sweat pouring from his giant's brow. *What is that thing?*

Freaked by his audience, the Cockatrice locked eyes onto Renard. It lurched forward and snapped its beak. Renard leapt backward, a look of horror on his face. *Why did it attack?*

La Roue chuckled. *This was almost the perfect start to the morning but alas, no.* He pulled a bag out of his pocket – it contained a fine, vermillion red powder. *The alchemist's special brew should keep the beast obedient for twelve hours. But by then, I'll be long gone. The Cockatrice, if it is still alive, will ravage Sirene as its counterpart did in Licorne whilst I'll be counting my gold in my private sanctum miles away.*

He took a handful of the red dust and blew it into the Cockatrice's face. The monster had no choice but to inhale it. It coughed and sneezed. The powder was fast-acting and the creature appeared stunned.

La Roue turned to Renard.

'As you can see, the Cockatrice is placid now. The Telliers did not pay for this premium service. You are wise to have supplemented, Renard. Most of the Telliers are now dead.'

'And you're sure this creature will kill the Gryphon? Your last Cockatrice was killed by a magician and his friends. If this one fails, I want my gold back,' Renard insisted.

You're so naïve. La Roue did his best to suppress mocking laughter. 'I'm afraid you did not read the terms and conditions of sale carefully enough.'

Renard's face dropped. 'What?'

'The contract clearly states that refunds are only available for repeat customers not first-time purchasers.' La Roue kept a straight face. *I love writing the small details.*

'But you have the contract. How can I check it?' Renard exclaimed.

Henrik shook his head. *La Roue always wins.*

La Roue laughed. *Idiots breed idiots. I'll never run out of clients.* 'But I will say this ... The magician was lucky in Licorne. Don't assume the same will happen again. With our alchemist's upgrades, this model of Cockatrice is the apex predator.' He knew which words and tone would soothe Renard's anxiety.

Renard did not feel reassured. *This had better work. I've cleaned out all my gold. If I don't get Gulliver's treasure, I'm ruined.* He caught sight of something running towards them with great urgency. 'Who's that?'

La Roue turned and smirked. *And Arcana provides the most ironic gift.*

Maubert was panting and afraid to talk. He was unsure how to tell La Roue the bad news. *I hope he's not too angry.* Then, he saw the Cockatrice in all in its horror. *What heresy and blasphemy has created such a beast?*

La Roue subtly nodded towards Renard. He understood the command. He snapped his fingers. 'Kill him!'

The Cockatrice sprinted forward and sliced the priest open with a single slash of its draconic talons. It gorged itself peeling skin then flesh from bone. It took time to enjoy his soft organs. This was the first proper meal it had eaten in weeks.

La Roue cracked a sickeningly smile. *You've outlived your usefulness, Maubert.*

Renard was simultaneously pleased and disgusted. Henrik never wanted to eat again; his stomach queasy from witnessing such vicious disembowelment. Behind the barrels, Talitha could not watch. She wanted to run but knew she could not or she would face the same fate as Maubert. She had no choice but to pull herself together. *No! I must follow La Roue. The others can handle themselves.*

Henrik tapped Renard's shoulder. 'Are you sure about this?'

I have no choice now. I signed a contract. Renard looked inland towards the Gryphon's lair that lay beyond them in the woods. He clenched his fist so hard that it started to tremble. *I'll steal your treasure, Gulliver. I will be the superior captain!* 'Come!'

Renard began walking to his destiny. The Cockatrice slowly and obediently stalked behind its new master. Henrik deliberately kept himself behind the monster from where he could keep an eye on it; he did not trust its loyalty.

La Roue looked over the still, calm La Mer Étroite. *I've got my gold. My work here is almost done. I've only got one more thing to do.* The sailors conducted their cleaning of the gruesome mess that was all the Cockatrice had left of Maubert. They took his remains and threw them into the water. *His death will be pinned on Renard. After all, he owns the murder weapon.*

La Roue snapped his fingers. His perception-altering field now activated, he started to walk back into town carefree and without fear of being spotted. Talitha was astounded. *I can still see him. Marie's spell worked! Wait? He's not boarding his ship, is he? He just killed the local priest and he's staying in town.* She rubbed her hands together. *La Roue thinks he's untouchable because of his spells. Well, time for his wheel to stop turning. This is going to be one of my most satisfying heists.*

The Streets of Sirene

I need to be smart. I need to be quick. La Roue could disappear at any moment.

Talitha kept close to La Roue but always out of sight. The vial of invisibility potion was ready in her palm. *I must drink this before he enters The Humming Mermaid. I need to sneak into his room and swipe his ledger when his guard is down.* She needed La Roue distracted to give her time to let the potion take effect. *Come on! Come on! Someone, something give me a chance!*

La Roue stopped in front of the Church of Arcana. *Maubert was a fool. Now he's dead. I've poisoned the heart of this town. Maubert was my fool.* He could not help but smile.

Here's my chance. Talitha snuck into an alley. With the leverage of a single finger, she removed the cork from the vial and downed the colourless solution in one. A minute passed. Nothing happened. She held up her hands and they were still visible. *Come on, come on, I need you to work.* She looked down at her legs and saw her knees start to blur. *It's working!* Limb after limb, she started to vanish. Her clothes vanished too. She was truly invisible. *Who needs perception-altering spells when you have good, old-fashioned potions?*

Yet, being invisible was not as easy as she expected. She needed to be vigilant. If she stepped into a muddy puddle, the water appeared to splash of its own accord; if she knocked into people they thought they were being attacked by invisible spirits – and the last thing she wanted to do was to start a panic. But she couldn't stop a stray dog barking. It could smell her even if it couldn't see her. Luckily for her, no-one paid any attention to stray dogs and she learnt to move through the streets unnoticed.

Finally, La Roue arrived at The Humming Mermaid. Talitha needed to dash in after him or she would lose him. She kept close behind him, matching his speed and stride; she was fortunate the wooden stairs and landing did not creak. *Thank goodness it's quiet here in the morning. I don't have to push past anyone.*

At the far end of the corridor, La Roue arrived at his room – a home from home. He put the key into the lock and with a single turn of the wrist, unlocked the door and pushed it open.

Talitha darted in before the door had time to close. *I need to hide!* She crouched in the corner plotting her next move. *What now? My potion will wear off within ten minutes. I have a dagger but I don't know what La Roue is capable of. I must be patient. Wait for the perfect moment to strike.*

La Roue placed his ledger on a specifically requested wooden writing desk. He was The Humming Mermaid's most loyal patron; he commanded significant sway and a piece of parchment together with a feather quill and a small pot of ink had been put out ready for him. He took a seat and picked up the quill, ready to begin.

Is he seriously writing a letter? To whom? Is that why he came back to the inn? What could be so important?

La Roue glared at the paper. He was not ready to pen his letter. *I need time to compose my thoughts.* He left the room and closed the door behind him, locking it with a turn of the key. The clunk of the lock turning was Talitha's signal.

Here's my chance! She sprang to her feet. The ledger was crying out to be stolen. *This is like stealing from a baby – a pompous, arrogant baby.*

She swiped the ledger from the desk.

Now the door! Talitha pulled out a small, invisible lock-pick from her pocket. It was a simple lock to pick. It was child's play. She opened the door, ran out of the room and as a final insult left the door deliberately ajar.

Minutes later, La Roue came back to his room whistling. He stopped dead when he saw the open door. *I closed and locked that. Why is it ajar?* He pushed the door, which swung open quietly and slowly, its hinges creaking. His eyes were drawn to his ledger's absence. *No!* He madly searched through his belongings, throwing sheets and personal items across the floor. *WHERE IS IT?*

But he found nothing. *I've been tricked.* And he knew exactly who tricked him. *Batel. You dare declare war against me? Against Arcana's Shadow? Have you forgotten who you are?*

He sat down and picked up the quill on the desk. *I was about to write to him, but the content of that letter has just changed and he will not like what I have to say to him now.*

11 – Le Choc des Rivaux

The Cockatrice stomped through the streets. People ran clear, screaming. Once they found a safe house, they slammed their doors shut, bolted them firmly and put furniture against them to reinforce them. Feral cats, their tails on high alert, hissed like snakes at the creature, and dogs barked, their teeth bared, before fleeing down alleys and diving into any refuge they could find. Rats dared not to scurry across the street.

The Cockatrice stopped before a puddle. It beheld its reflection and, although it still recognised its own face, it hated what it saw. It was a far cry from the rooster that once patrolled its coop. It growled at its abominable reflection and slammed its draconic talons into the puddle sending water flying in all directions.

'Keep calm.' Renard's rough voice was hardly soothing, but the Cockatrice bowed its head and obeyed. Renard grinned; he enjoyed the power he held over the creature as he enjoyed the oppressive fear the Cockatrice instilled. *A good captain should inspire fear and loyalty in his crew.*

Henrik lurked behind his master, his thoughts elsewhere. *I've got until midday. Take the gold and leave. You can find a saner employer – one that doesn't dabble in the bizarre.*

The Cockatrice jerked its head to one side; its nose had picked up a foul, mortifying stench. It wanted to lash out, but La Roue's alchemical powder was still suppressing its wild, destructive nature. Frustrated, it clawed at the ground with talons so sharp that they cut through the stone.

'What is it? What's wrong?' Renard was lost for ideas.

Henrik turned and saw the source of irritation, not only for the Cockatrice, but also himself. Johan blocked the road out of the village which lay on the route towards the Gryphon's lair, his two enchanted swords already drawn. Johan smirked. His itch for battle was about to be scratched. *So Renard has played his hand.* Excitedly, he pointed his right sword at the foul beast. 'We meet again, treasonous poultry.'

The Cockatrice hissed and barked, tossing its head furiously from side to side. La Roue's powder was starting to fail and, unknown to Renard and Henrik, who exchanged nervous glances, its nose was filled with the magical stench of its kin.

'You smell your brother on this sword, don't you chicken? These are the swords that slayed him!'

The Cockatrice stormed forth, its bulging muscular hind legs building up tremendous speed. It charged recklessly, its draconic instincts no longer suppressed, and slammed its rooster-head into Johan's chest. The giant was sent flying and crashed into a wooden cart. It broke under his weight, splinters sent flying, sharp edges breaking skin. He coughed and wheezed. But soon, despite the blood that trickled down his face, he started laughing. For he had left a parting shot. He had driven one of his enchanted blades into the Cockatrice's neck.

The creature cried and howled in agony and Renard wanted to pull the sword free, but Henrik held him back. He would be ripped apart by the Cockatrice's flailing claws. Not that help was needed. The Cockatrice's magical defences activated in response to the blade's presence and expelled it. The blade clattered on to the road and the bloody wound healed then disappeared.

Renard's eyes lit up. 'Fantastic!'

The Cockatrice was ready for more. Johan jumped back on to his feet and wielded his swords again. The creature locked eyes with its assailant.

Henrik cracked his knuckles. 'Leave Johan to me.'

'Why?' Renard felt his satisfaction cut off.

'You need to get to your treasure,' Henrik reminded his employer. *He's right. I must keep moving.* Renard whistled and the Cockatrice's violent gaze broke from Johan. The smuggler captain waved the beast to the south and reluctantly it obeyed. Head down, it stomped forward. Renard followed on behind and as they passed the surprised giant, he spat at his feet.

Johan laughed. *That pride will be your downfall.* He wiped a trickle of blood from his cheek and picked up his enchanted sword. The taste of iron readied him for his true fight.

'A thank you would be nice,' goaded Henrik as he brought up the rear of the unusual exodus.

'For what?' Johan became prickly in defence.

'Saving your life.'

Johan growled. Years of anger and hatred would not be quelled so easily. 'Come on. Draw your swords.'

Henrik sighed. 'How many times have we fought, Johan? I just want to talk about what happened all those years ago.' Henrik legitimately did not want this fight. They had fought over and over. He was beginning to think now was the time for reconciliation.

But Johan refused to engage with such feelings. 'I was a proud warrior, husband and father. I trusted you once, Henrik. But in your idiocy, you sold out our people. Now, we wander Etellia, a foreign country to the west of our true home, rebuilding ourselves. For that reason, we must fight again.'

Henrik sighed. *Very well.* He drew his swords from their sheaths. His blades were rusting and heavily dented. 'Did your cleric friend gave you those shining swords?'

Johan limbered up his body. 'I found my purpose, Henrik. I am a monster hunter. You can do what you've always done, bounce from criminal to criminal, but leave me to my chosen path.'

Henrik cracked his neck. 'So be it.'

They wound up their arm muscles and swung their blades.

'BRING IT ON!'

Johan charged in first and they clashed. The clang of metal reverberated through the still air. Little finesses or elegancy was on display. This was visceral and personal. Intense. Quickly, both dropped the formalities of battle and cast their swords aside; the former allies, for all their loathing, would never maim or kill each other, merely beat the snot out of each other. They locked their large, hairy hands together and pushed hard against the thought of losing; their full strength exerted. Faces as red as the blood that pulsed inside them, their muscles trembled violently. Neither would back down. They refused to. They screamed and roared instead.

Both giants lost their footing. They slipped. Hands unlocked. They both bounced back onto their feet.

Johan threw the first punch.

He missed.

Henrik jabbed back striking Johan's shoulder and then his upper chest forcing him back. Before he had time to recover, Henrik slammed his kneecap into Johan's groin.

But he did not yield. He remained standing despite the pain. He laughed. 'Is that it?'

'I just want to talk.' Henrik pleaded.

Johan wiped the saliva dripping from his mouth. 'I'm not listening.'

Henrik growled with growing frustration. 'Why won't you take this seriously? Why won't you accept my apology?'

'Because that's what you want! And I'm not going to give it to you!'

Johan bent forward and charged in. Henrik could not stop the incoming tackle. He let the contact happen. Punch after punch, Henrik tried to push him off, but it did little to arrest Johan's momentum and he was driven backward. With a dull thud, he slammed into a stone wall; its reaction force punched him hard. He howled in pain but kept thrashing Johan's back with his fists until eventually Johan's grip around his waist faltered. Henrik was no longer pinned against the wall; he managed to push himself free.

A single blow across the face and Johan's jawline stretched. He had to pause and catch his breath. *I'm spitting blood.*

Both panted heavily.

'Why punch me the other day in the bar if all you wanted was to talk?' Johan gasped.

'It's how we say hello nowadays.'

Johan laughed. 'At least we agree on something.'

He threw another punch. Henrik staggered backward.

'How many? How many times must I say sorry, Johan? I did not mean for your family to get hurt.'

'You say it until you mean it, Henrik.' Johan landed the toughest blow.

Henrik was stunned. *I do mean it. Why does he think I don't?*

'You've not learnt from your mistakes.'

Henrik denied the truth. 'What about you? You think that a magician and cleric can replace what you've lost.'

'I protect people from monsters. The bounty I collect isn't just for me, but to rebuild our home someday.'

Henrik saw a flicker of hope. *He's got a purpose. He needs gold.* 'Then let me help you!'

'No! Until you play it straight, I will not accept a single coin from you.'

Johan calmed himself. 'I side with those who fight the monsters. You always side with those controlling them!'

Henrik had heard enough. He threw his fist. Johan knocked it away with his left arm and crafted his winning shot – a swift uppercut slammed into his fellow giant's chin. Henrik's jaw vibrated as the force of the blow made his skull shudder. Dazed and dizzy, he staggered then fell to the ground.

Johan stood over his defeated rival; took pity. *The world is complex, Henrik. Sometimes we must work with those we do not agree with to achieve our goals. I accept the path I tread will have bumps. I believe I have chosen correctly.*

Slowly but surely, he picked up his enchanted swords and trudged back to The Humming Mermaid. *Batel, Marie and Talitha – we shall drink together in victory this evening.*

12 – Le Nouveau Maître

The Gryphon's Cave

Playing with one's food is a cruel and malicious trait. But for the Gryphon, it was part of its breakfast ritual. It dangled a roughed-up grey squirrel over its open mouth. The squirrel squirmed as it stared into the abyss of the Gryphon's throat. Without a second thought, the Gryphon dropped the squirrel and swallowed it whole.

Now, it settled down to business.

After all, it had visitors.

This had better work. Carla readied her arrows.

Marie trembled before what she could not deny was the magnificent, if malicious, grace of the creature. *Its eyes are soulful.* 'I thought Gryphons were noble creatures in legend. Why is it content to live amongst smugglers?'

Batel positioned his halberd ready to generate an escape portal if needed. 'There's honour amongst thieves. It enjoyed life with Gulliver and Isaac rather being locked up in a castle vault.'

Slowly, the Gryphon approached but only to Isaac, who was not afraid and greeted the beast as an old friend.

'It's been too long.' Isaac tended to the Gryphon's feathers and stroked its face. The creature welcomed the friendly touch; everyone else it encountered recently wanted to murder it. With his fingertips, Isaac ran a line across the scars beneath the creature's neck. The lion section of its body had been forcibly fused to its eagle-head by what he knew was horrifying, experimental alchemy. *It must have hurt. No wonder you're so vicious. I can't imagine what torture does to the mind.*

'Father's dead,' Isaac whispered solemnly.

The Gryphon grew mournful and hung its head.

Isaac brushed himself down. 'I ... I will be your new master.'

The creature shook its head. It dismissed the notion immediately and its reaction broke Isaac's heart. He could not speak. *Am I not worthy? I'll ... I'll never be my father.*

Marie's heart empathised. *He's crushed.* 'You would make a fine master,' she said as she placed a comforting hand on his shoulder.

But standing on the sidelines, Carla had noticed the Gryphon's gaze had not averted from Batel. *The Gryphon has already made its choice.* 'It wants you, halberd boy.'

'You? The magician?' Isaac swallowed back the tears.

The Gryphon allowed Isaac one last stroke. He accepted the invitation. *I'll miss your soft feathers.* Then he turned to Batel. 'What are you planning to do?'

The magician took his time. *That's a difficult one to answer.* Carla was eager to learn too, yet Marie took a step back. *Arcana guides me, but Batel has little faith in her, so I will keep my counsel.*

Batel paced the ground. 'I am committed to kill the monsters that mankind has created. As to why, you can trust my conviction.'

Carla felt sadness in his words. *That's as honest and open as he's going to be. Something dreadful must have happened.*

Isaac went to shield the Gryphon, but the beast did not seem to want protection. It acknowledged its destiny and respected Batel's resolve to carry it out. There was intelligence here.

Batel found himself torn. *I promised myself that I would slay the engineered monsters I encountered. The Gryphon is no different to a Cockatrice – two monsters forged together against their will. It should not exist.* He inhaled deeply. *This Gryphon is strong. Arcana's Shadow will manufacture stronger beasts that will be even harder for us to kill.*

We'll need all the help we can get. He mustered the courage to explain. 'We haven't got a choice. I believe the Gryphon also hates its fellow monsters ... Am I right?'

The creature bellowed in agreement. It then bowed its head in acceptance. Batel beheld the beast. *Like me, you were cast out into the world on a different path to the one from which you were raised.* He looked deep into the creatures' knowing eyes. *Why am I feeling a connection to this monster?* His fingers were fidgeting constantly, tapping the staff of his halberd.

'I need allies to help me, it is true. But I always thought they would be human. Maybe to achieve my goal, I need to grow. A Gryphon can take on monsters by itself.'

Carla could not remain silent. 'You can't be serious! That Gryphon has killed people! Why are you being a hypocrite?'

'Carla!' Marie snapped.

'It's OK, Marie.' Batel signalled to her to stand down. He turned to Carla. 'You're more than welcome to kill it ... if you can.'

Carla froze. *That's not fair. You know that none of us can stop the Gryphon on our own.*

'If we stop Renard and Isaac removes the treasure, the Gryphon will leave for the mountains,' Batel reasoned.

'Can you guarantee that?' Carla remained stern.

The Gryphon bowed its head. The beast had its own honour. As much as it enjoyed the free supply of food, its eagle-heart longed for the steep hills and cloudy peaks it inhabited prior to its monstrous transformation.

I hope this gamble pays off, Batel. Carla sighed. 'Very well.'

'Johan can't delay Renard for long,' Marie reminded all the urgency of the situation.

'Are you ready?' Batel asked the Gryphon.

It nodded once.

'Good! Let us prepare!'

13 – La Folie du Passeur

Renard reached the path's end with a boastful swagger. He turned up his nose at the sight of Batel, Marie and Carla, who he saw standing outside The Gryphon's cave. *Of course they're here.* He looked around for the creature but could not see it. *Is it hiding?* Then, he clocked Isaac's presence. *So Gulliver's runt has dared to show his face.* The Cockatrice stomped along a few paces behind him. Carla and Isaac both stared open-mouthed at the beast. *Who would make such a thing?* The creature crowed once; this was its morning for slaughter.

Batel, his fears confirmed, moved to the front of the group. *La Roue must have sold him a spare Cockatrice whilst the price was low.* His halberd blade started to glow its trademark faint lilac in preparation for the worst.

'We've already had our first conquest. Maubert was his name, wasn't it?' Renard boasted.

'You killed Maubert?' Carla exclaimed. Marie closed her eyes. *May your soul return to the Earth into Arcana's grace. May she forgive you and help heal your ailing heart.*

Batel smiled reassuringly at Marie. 'Are you ready?' he whispered.

'Yes.' Marie cleared her mind.

Renard regarded the three of them, waiting for them to put up some form of defence. When nothing happened, he shook his head in disbelief and snapped his fingers. 'Kill them!'

On his command, the Cockatrice tramped forward, eager to obey the command. But as it did so, Marie raised her staff and a blinding light flashed forth from the orb. Batel, Isaac and Carla covered their eyes to protect them from its impact, but in that moment Renard and the Cockatrice were blinded. The Cockatrice roared and screeched in protest. Sangterre in the orb continued to churn. Magical energy erupted as strings of white light wrapped themselves around the Cockatrice's feet and bound themselves into the Earth. The Cockatrice looked down at its feet. It was stuck. It tried to break free but could not. It tried to pull itself free with its beak, but the strings of light which bound it were impervious to its attacks. The beast let out a terrified screech that travelled for miles and summoned forth the Gryphon from inside its cave. It recognised Renard and glared at him and his wretched companion in disgust.

There it is. Renard found it surprising how easily it stood beside his enemies. *The Gryphon has sided with Isaac.*

'Renard!' Isaac called out. 'What happened to my father? Why are you wearing his jacket?'

Renard sneered. *Hasn't he figured it out yet?* 'I want that treasure, boy.'

'You can't have it. It is stolen property. It should be returned to Mercia to its owner,' Marie told him. She slammed her staff into the ground – *surely as a cleric of Arcana, I must have some sway?*

Renard hooted. 'You think it will be returned to the people who lost it? That gold will disappear into blind pockets quicker than you blink. It's better in my hands.'

The Cockatrice sensed the Gryphon's superiority and bared its beak. Incensed, it found a new strength and heaved its magical binds out of the earth one by one.

'Fantastic!' Renard marvelled.

The Cockatrice charged in. The Gryphon reared, ready to pounce, but the Cockatrice was too fast for it and slashed its exposed chest. In retaliation, the Gryphon dug its talons into the Cockatrice's shoulders and bit into its neck. The Cockatrice wailed as it struggled, but the Gryphon would not let go. The Cockatrice tensed its barbed tail and swished and swiped it into the Gryphon's face.

The Gryphon instinctively let go.

Both beasts pulled back. The scratches and open wounds magically healed over. Their stamina, built from the Sangterre coursing through their veins, was being tested.

'Good!' Renard cheered his contender on.

The Gryphon glanced towards Batel seeking his support. It would only fight if it had the magician's word.

'What? It's listening to you?' Renard scoffed.

Batel bit his tongue. *The Gryphon is testing me.* But he swallowed his pride. *We've gambled on the Gryphon to succeed.* He nodded once at the Gryphon. It accepted the signal.

'You two suit each other,' Renard jabbed.

Batel growled. Marie elbowed him to remind him she was there if he needed her.

'Don't listen to him,' she murmured.

'The pompous beast and the arrogant magician struggling together ... I say you'll die together!' Renard laughed. *I'm enjoying this. They must listen to me! They must respect me!*

'Ready your bow,' Batel whispered to Carla.

She nodded. She had her bow already loaded, hidden, lowered by her knee. All she had to do was raise it and then fire when the perfect shot presented itself.

Renard could not resist another jibe. 'The Gryphon's rejected you, Isaac. You're nothing without daddy now, are you?'

Isaac scowled. 'What happened to my father?'

Renard sniggered. 'You know your father was partial to a few drinks at sea, Isaac ... well, he said things, rude things about me. Insulting my worth. Said I would never be a captain. So, one night, when the booze loosened his tongue, I stabbed him!'

Isaac froze. The news he had been dreading was true. Marie placed a reassuring hand on the young man's shoulder. Batel and the Gryphon growled concurrently.

'You coward!' Carla labelled with disgust.

'I threw him overboard and took his captain's jacket for my own ... Fits me rather well, don't you think, Isaac?' Renard twisted the knife further.

The red mist descended. Isaac stormed towards Renard winding up a soft punch, but Batel blocked him with his halberd. 'Let me at him! He killed my father!'

'And the Cockatrice? You'll be eaten before you even reach him.'

Isaac refused to listen. 'LET ME THROUGH!'

Marie acted quickly. Two magical binds shot out of the orb on her staff. They wrapped around his feet and locked him to the ground.

'NO!!' Isaac tried to free himself, lifting his legs, or trying to, then defeated, he bent down and tugged at the binds with his bare hands in a vain attempt to pull them out of the Earth.

Marie went to pacify him. 'Isaac! Listen to me!'

'He killed my father!' he raged, fists flailing at Renard.

Marie broke convention and abandoned her training. She did what she felt was right. She hugged him. Tightly. And stroked his hair. She disarmed him with care and attention. 'It's OK ... it's OK.' His body, first tense, relaxed as his rage faded. He wept in despair. Marie did not let go. *Let Batel handle this.*

'Let him weep!' Renard boasted.

'Now!' Batel whispered to Carla.

Marie knew what was coming. *Make it quick.*

The Cockatrice charged in again. The Gryphon defended its ground. It swiped its claw into the Cockatrice's face and knocked the beast off its stride.

'Get up!' Renard ordered. 'Fight for your-'

Something pierced Renard's shoulder. He staggered. Metal dug into his flesh. His eyes quivered from shock. *An arrow?* He looked up. *You!!*

Carla lowered her bow. 'You're the weak link!'

Weak link? How dare you? Renard refused to give up. 'Get them!' he shouted at the Cockatrice.

His creature lurched itself onto its feet and crowed its battle cry, but the Gryphon's trumpeting roar silenced the beast. Wary now, it stepped back.

Why are you backing down? Renard dared not pull the arrow out of his shoulder for fear he would bleed to death. *What do I do? I can't be captured. I'd rot in a jail. I won't be hanged.*

The Gryphon had other ideas. It stepped forward as Batel read the charge sheet. 'You killed its master. You betrayed your captain. You murdered a father.'

Marie buried Isaac's head into her shoulder. *You should not see this. You must remain innocent.* She closed her eyes against what was about to happen next.

Renard whimpered and backed himself against a tree. He knew what was coming. As the Gryphon charged at him, he even laughed to think he was meeting the same end as the pathetic Maubert.

In one efficient slash, the Gryphon ripped open Renard's neck. He was dead within a heartbeat. Yet if the others thought the creature would gorge on its kill, it chose not to feast on the smuggler. It did not wish to consume tainted meat. It roared a sombre horn. It honoured its former master.

'It's done,' Marie whispered.

Isaac lifted his head from her shoulder, saw Renard's body on the ground and breathed a sigh of relief. *Father ... I hope you can rest more easily now.* He turned to Batel and nodded his thanks.

Batel nodded in return. He accepted responsibility for this grizzly affair. *We've walked in the shadows to defeat those lurking within. These monsters La Roue sells have Sangterre in their heart – the magic of the earth, nature, even Arcana herself. But nature can be cruel and merciless. The Gryphon has its own justice.* He turned towards the Gryphon. 'It's time to finish it.'

The Gryphon bellowed.
It set eyes on the Cockatrice.

14 – La Fierté du Gryphon

The Gryphon beat its wings and took to the sky.

The Cockatrice tried to copy its mortal enemy but its wings were not strong enough to achieve full flight. It was not designed for such privilege. It was designed as a ground beast but with draconic wings as an extra layer of intimidation. But right now it was intimidating no-one.

The Gryphon dived down and planted its front claws on its opponent's rooster-head. The Cockatrice was pinned to the ground and The Gryphon tore into its flesh – a deep wound formed, exposing the central Sangterre vein – the magical lifeline that held the fusion between chicken and dragon in harmony. There was an anguished crow for mercy, but the Gryphon possessed none. Before the wound healed, the Gryphon drank from the Sangterre vein – a delicious, nutritious meal which would reinforce its own harmony. The Cockatrice flailed and gasped as its lifeforce was siphoned away. Without the precious Sangterre, the fusion between chicken and dragon came apart at the seam; the rooster-head detached from the dragon-body and rolled across the ground towards its foolish master.

The Gryphon turned to Batel. It had its executed its task dutifully. Batel nodded in appreciation.

It gave one final glanced towards Isaac, who bowed his head in respect, and the Gryphon breathed in a new freedom, its task complete. It beat its wings and took to the skies to find a new home; its heart yearned for the mountains. As it ascended, it circled its allies – a final farewell before it became no more than a silhouette against the sunlit sky.

As Batel watched it fly away, he knew they would meet again. *It won't forget me.*

Carla watched on, unsettled; troubled. *That beast killed good friends and yet we're letting it go.* 'Are you sure this was a good idea?'

'It was the best we could do given the circumstances. Not everything works out perfectly every time, Carla. Sometimes, we must accept compromise.'

Carla did not answer. She needed time to process and to reflect.

Marie tended to Isaac. 'Are you alright?'

'Yes.' Isaac spoke with calm. *I'm glad it's over.*

The orb in Marie's staff glistened; the magical bindings holding Isaac to the ground evaporated into dust.

'Thank you. I almost got myself killed, didn't I?'

Marie smiled at his sincerity. She was at her happiest when she helped people.

Isaac cleared his throat; he felt it was important to speak. 'My father said that Gryphon of legend responded to those whose hearts are strong in conviction and pure of cause. Whatever inspired you, Batel, the Gryphon responded to your heart. I wish you luck.'

Batel brushed away the compliment with the back of his hand, but Isaac's tale did ring true. *The Gryphon has been in the heart of the factories operated by Arcana's Shadow. Deep down it must hate what it has become.*

Isaac entered the Gryphon's cave as the others followed. Amongst its bed of fallen branches woven together into a nest, were several large chests waiting to be opened. Carla's curiosity got the better of her and she lifted the lid on one of them. Gold coins and jewels spilled out – diamonds and rubies, sapphires and emeralds, their colours sparkling in the half-light of the cave. Her eyes glistened with the gleam of gold. *No wonder Renard killed for this.*

'What do we do with it all?' Marie asked.

'Renard was right,' Carla thought aloud. 'The Mercians will steal it. It won't go back to the people it was originally stolen from.'

Batel knew their opinions did not matter. 'It's down to Isaac what happens.'

Isaac sighed. 'I'm no smuggler. I want a legitimate business. I want to found a proper shipping business, a trade company.'

Everyone nodded and Batel walked up to him and placed his hand on his shoulder. 'Be better than what came before. Be different to your father.'

Marie found the comment strange. *There's a personal undertone there. It's as if Batel passed a dream onto Isaac that he can no longer achieve himself.*

'Thank you. I'll leave some gold for Sirene. For all the trouble,' Isaac offered.

Carla appreciated the gesture. *It's the least he can do.*

He turned to the others. 'And take some gold for your journey. You'll need to feed and find resources for yourselves.'

'We won't take too much,' Marie promised.

'Once we're done, I want to say goodbye to Talitha,' Isaac requested.

Marie gladly smiled. 'We can arrange that.'

The Humming Mermaid - Sirene

Johan's aching face made talking and even drinking slow. He slumped in his seat in the bar as he let the numbness set in. *Henrik still packs a wallop.* He took a gulp from his glass and winced. The froth of the beer stuck to his beard. But the alcohol would numb his pain and he was grateful to be back at base. *Peace and quiet.*

'JOHAN!' Talitha screeched across the room; her invisibility potion long worn off.

Johan sat up pretending to be alert. *Why does she sound like a screeching bell? Ten minutes of quiet, is that too much to ask?*

She inspected the bruises on his face. 'Are you OK? You look like a punched potato.'

'You should have seen Henrik. He looked like a squished turd.' Johan finished his pint of ale. He suppressed a burp. 'Did you succeed this morning?'

Talitha nodded proudly. 'The ledger is secure.'

Johan smiled. 'Well done. Batel will be eager to read it.'

Talitha took her seat opposite him. She placed her bestiary on the table and opened it. She was keen to add to the entries with her enchanted quill. She merrily scribbled away, happily humming to herself. Johan sat still. It hurt to move even a single muscle. He stared at the cracked ceiling, not thinking deeply about anything, just letting the day wash over him. *I need another beer.*

The next thing he knew Talitha kicked his shin. He broke his dozing gaze and glared furiously. *What now?* Talitha sensed trouble and flashed a glance across the room. His eyes followed hers.

La Roue was approaching them.

His eyes went immediately to Talitha's notebook. *That's not my ledger.* Inspecting the crude drawing of the Gryphon, La Roue hid a smirk. *I have found the correct people.* 'Excuse me. Are you the associates of the purple-robed magician, Batel?'

Talitha slammed her notebook shut. *He's onto us.*

Johan exhaled heavily. *I'm not in the mood for another fight, but let's see what we can do.* He took to his feet. The giant loomed over the salesman. 'What if we are his associates?'

He stinks of beer and blood. La Roue backstepped, repulsed. He forced an envelope into Johan's hand. In return, Johan belched into La Roue's face. La Roue coughed violently, suppressing the urge to vomit and fled quickly before the giant could do anything more to him. This was turning out to be one of the worst days of his life.

Talitha sniggered. *Serves him right.*

'He was lucky I didn't pick him up and toss him out into the mud.' Johan sat down pleased with himself. *Slimy little toad.* He inspected the name Batel' written in elegant calligraphy on the envelope La Roue had given him. 'He writes better than you do, Talitha.'

'Hey!' Talitha tried to snatch the letter, but Johan moved it out of reach. He folded his arms and relaxed. 'It's not addressed to you.'

Talitha puffed out her cheeks in annoyance. But she did not object. *Can't be too nosy.*

'But what does it say?'

'It's for Batel's eyes only.' Johan's smile betrayed his concerns. *La Roue is up to something. This was his parting shot. Batel ... what have we provoked?*

15 – Les Secrets du Grand Livre

Outside The Humming Mermaid - Sirene

Isaac straightened his jacket as he waited outside the inn. Despite the treasure that lined his pockets, he felt neither rich nor important. *Be brave, Isaac. She's only a girl.* He looked expectantly at the bar door; he knew she would come.

Talitha appeared; her cheeks flushed. 'Is everything alright? I heard what happened. Sounds ... sounds-'

'Eventful.' Isaac found this word the best to describe the situation as he finished her sentence.

She laughed tentatively and nervously. She could barely keep eye contact. 'So you're going back to Mercia?'

'Yes. I've got a lot of hard work to do. Exciting, but tough.' Isaac swallowed. *Keep it together, Isaac.* 'And you? Are you off to hunt more monsters that lurk in the woods?'

'Yes. We're making good progress. We're close to a breakthrough, I think.' Talitha's excitement was clear.

Isaac respected her drive. *She's dedicated. She wants to see her mission through to the end. I cannot deny her the chance to finish it.* 'Well, we both need luck then.'

Isaac took her hand and kissed it. She felt something inside her stir. 'In a few years, once we've achieved more in our lives, I hope we meet again, Talitha.'

Such a gentleman. Talitha did not know what to do. She pecked his cheek with a brief kiss and ran back inside the inn. Isaac left for the docks with a spring in his step. *We've got an interesting path ahead of us, Talitha. Let's see where it takes us.*

Inside The Humming Mermaid

By the time a smiling Talitha returned to the bar, Batel, Marie and Johan had arrived and were installed at the table with Johan. Marie was tending to Johan's bruises with a special treatment her mother swore by. It stung.

'Stay still!' Marie protested.

'I've already been hurt enough today.' Johan moaned.

'And what about Henrik? What will he do now?' Marie dreaded to imagine the state of Henrik. *Must have been quite a brawl.*

'I left him unconscious. He'll flee and find new work.' Johan sounded disappointed. *The pattern will repeat. One day, we'll be able to talk.*

Meanwhile, Batel was spending his attention on La Roue's ledger. He sifted through page after page in frustration. *He's written in code. He's not even using the alphabet, just random symbols. It's going to take months if not years to decipher.* He snapped the ledger shut. *I thought I had something, a legitimate paper trail, but La Roue is too clever.*

Marie saw Batel's disappointment. 'Nothing?' *He had pinned a lot of hope on that book.*

'Nothing.'

'It will come to you.'

Carla entered the inn but she would not come over to join them. Instead, she hung back and signalled for Batel to come to her. Batel furrowed his brow. *Strange.* He stood up and went to meet her.

Marie rolled her eyes. *Attention seeker.*

'Is everything alright?' Batel asked.

'Sirene is in shock. People are mourning for Maubert.'

Batel understood her predicament. She was of Sirene but seen with outsiders. 'You know, we could use a good archer ... come with us?'

Carla smiled but shook her head. 'Sirene needs time to heal. I need to heal. I know Renard died, but the Gryphon simply flew away. I do not know if I can be put in that situation again. I'm not you.'

Batel understood. 'Very well ... But thank you for your help. We needed you.'

She smiled in return. 'You're on a strange road, Batel. The others trust you, but you're hiding something.'

'We all hide things.' Batel dodged a direct answer.

'You'll hurt someone. Lose people.'

'I'm sad to say I already have.'

Carla took a deep breath. 'Johan's a warrior. Talitha's a thief. But what about Marie? She's a pure heart guided by her faith. Why is she involved in this seedy business of hunting monsters?'

Batel took time to compose his answer. 'We all need an anchor that keeps us true and balanced when things get dark. Without Marie, we ... no, I might stray from the path.'

Carla looked over Batel's shoulder to see Marie treating Johan, and Talitha writing in her notebook. *They're an odd group but they function well together.* 'Listen. I need to let things in Sirene calm down and get back to normal. Then, maybe, I'll be ready to help you again.'

Batel accepted the polite refusal with a smile. 'OK. Take your time.'

'Well, farewell, halberd boy.' Carla left with a pained smile.

As he raised his hand to bid her goodbye, Batel thought it was a shame she was leaving. *She's strong, but you can't expect everyone to go along with you. I'm lucky in that Marie, Johan and Talitha are with me. Yet I sense that I will need to rely on Carla one day in the future.*

Silently, he returned to his friends.

'She's not joining us, is she?' Johan asked.

'No,' Batel answered, clearly disappointed.

'She'll find her way. We all do.' Marie continued to dab the wet cloth on Johan's bruises.

As Batel nodded in acceptance of this truth, Talitha saw Johan still gripping La Roue's letter. She despaired. 'You've not given him the letter, you lumbering oaf?'

'What letter?' Batel was confused.

Johan perked up. He passed the letter over. 'La Roue gave this to us. In return, I burped in his face.'

'JOHAN!' Marie hit Johan's bicep with his staff.

Talitha still laughed at La Roue's appalled expression. 'The creep deserved it.'

Batel studied the envelope in his hand and hesitated. *Do I open it? Of course I do, but do I really want to read its contents?* He sighed and opened it anyway, pulling out the letter. He unfolded the parchment and read silently; he had no intention of reading it aloud before checking the letter's contents.

'*Le Bateleur,*

I know you ordered the theft of my ledger. I commend your audacity. Your crusade against Arcana's Shadow, whilst admirable, is foolhardy. Do not forget your heritage. Like me, you are a child of the free market. Deny it all you want, but deep-down Arcana's Shadow is your family and your inheritance. I understand the fire that burns in your heart, but your foolishness ends now. You cannot hope to decipher my ledger's code. My cipher cannot be broken. Without me, you are a scared orphan playing hero with your enchanted halberd.

Bring the ledger, and come alone to La Colline Du Savant in one week's time. Do not disappoint me. Remember what I know. Remember where you came from.

La Roue.'

Immediately, Batel folded the letter and sealed it back into the envelope without comment.

'Aren't you going to tell us what he said?' Talitha squawked with surprise.

Marie found it strange. 'Are you OK?'

Johan saw Batel was lost in his thoughts. *La Roue has blindsided him. But with what?*

Batel was caught in two minds. *I should be pleased. This is a major victory. I've got a face-to-face meeting. La Roue is on the backfoot. The ledger is our bargaining chip. But I must be careful. La Roue plays dirty. He'll drag my name through the mud. My heritage will be shown in all its grotesque glory.* He pinched the skin on the bridge of his nose. *It's a risk I must take.*

'Speak to us,' Marie said. 'What do we do?'

Batel composed himself.

'La Roue is my responsibility. I do not wish for any of you to deal with him.' *La Colline Du Savant?* Batel mapped out the next leg of their quest. 'If I were a gambler, I would wager Arcana's Shadow would be based on an island somewhere off the coast. There is an archipelago to the west, on the edge of La Mer Étroite, which might be worth investigating.'

All agreed.

Johan laughed. 'I'm sure we'll run into trouble.'

'Who knows? We might bump into the Gryphon again,' Marie pondered. *Arcana does work in a mysterious way. I believe she is guiding us even if Batel refuses to acknowledge her.*

The clock in the corner struck the hour and Talitha looked up from her bestiary. All the while they were talking, Talitha had been adding the last details to the entry on the Gryphon. In her mind, another leg of her grand adventure was completed.

Now, she wrote the last sentence:

And so ends the tale of the Gulliver's Gryphon.

The Zoharian Bladers Series

The angel Zerachiel faces the most daunting of challenges. He must confront an old enemy who will set loose hell's fire upon his enemies. Lose and the city of Rumon will be owned by the demons and their nefarious Fallen Angel masters. He is expected to win. Heaven expects. The Archangels expects, no, demand victory!

Check out the first entry of this epic fantasy trilogy- **The Successor of Ramiel** – on all good online booksellers.

Bestiary Index

- **Arcana** – A goddess of life and death who has a nationwide religion worshipping her.
- **Arcana's Shadow** – A mysterious organisation that creates monsters.
- **Batel's Halberd** – An enchanted halberd that can create portals by slicing the air.
- **Cleric of Arcana** – A travelling member of the Church of Arcana bringing peace and goodwill to all people.
- **Cockatrice** – A monster made by fusing a rooster's head and a dragon's body.
- **Elixir** – Potions carried by Marie that restore health and stamina.
- **Invisibility Potion** – A tool Talitha uses to assist her stealing/infiltrations.
- **Johan's Blades** – Enchanted swords made using Sangterre.
- **Licorne** – A town that is obsessed with unicorns.
- **Marie's Staff** – A wooden staff with an orb of Sangterre at the top. It can create magical barriers, blinding light and learn new spells.
- **Mirror Shield** – A reflective shield that was commissioned by Matto to slay the Cockatrice.
- **Talitha's Daggers** – Enchanted daggers made using Sangterre.
- **Sangterre** – A mysterious fluid that allows mankind to conjure spells.
- **Tellier Family** – A noble family that is the most important political force in Licorne.

- **Tellier Purchase Order** – A document detailing the order of the Cockatrice.
- **Unicorn** – Magical creatures whose blood is rich in Sangterre.

Author Notes

The Arcana's Bestiary Series is the result of my curious look into heraldry and I wanted to construct a world where such creatures were suddenly dropped into an unsuspecting world. I chose the Cockatrice and the Gryphon because of the bizarre yet terrifying potential it presented. I hope you've enjoyed what I've created.

I would like to thank everyone who have supported me. This project means a lot to me and I'm eternally appreciative for their help. If you enjoyed this book, please leave a review on the page where you bought the book. Reviews help to spread the word, especially for independent authors.

Milton Keynes UK
Ingram Content Group UK Ltd.
UKHW010711080823
426520UK00001B/80